THE BLUE
HALLELUJAH

ANDY STRAKA

Cedar Creek Publishing
Virginia, USA

Cover Images
(Front) Thinkstock/Comstock
(Back) Thinkstock/iStock

978-0-9891465-9-3

Cedar Creek Publishing
Virginia, USA
www.cedarcreekauthors.com
Twitter @VirginiaBooks
Facebook.com/CedarCreekPublishing

The Blue Hallelujah

FRANK PAVLICEK MYSTERIES
A Witness Above
A Killing Sky
Cold Quarry
The Night Falconer
Flightfall
The K Street Hunting Society

DRAGONFLIES SERIES
Dragonflies: Shadow of Drones
Dragonflies: Visible Means

SUSPENSE
Record Of Wrongs
The Blue Hallelujah

For more information visit www.andystraka.com
Twitter @AndyStraka
Facebook.com/Andy.Straka

Justitiae soror fides.

Prologue

All afternoon the old man has been sweltering in the steamy woods, watching and waiting, wondering if he can pull it off. All afternoon with a pit in his stomach, sweat dripping from his brow onto his dark clothing, flies and mosquitoes biting and swirling.

He has lost track of how many times he's raised the binoculars to his eyes, struggling to keep a focus on the girl.

Not much stirs in the late afternoon heat. Central Virginia is even more of a broiler this time of year than DC. He wishes he were home. Seeing the girl and being in Richmond again only brings back memories, making his dilemma more real.

He glances at his watch. Time will be running out soon. In a few minutes the day camp is scheduled to break up for the afternoon, and a line of parents in their cars will start forming along the entrance road.

The girl, he knows from watching, can be a bit of a loner. Maybe he'll be able to slip behind one of the restrooms and grab her without being noticed, but it will mean taking a big risk.

The children are being herded into loosely organized groups. Counselors only keep close track of the younger ones, and near pandemonium erupts as the kids burn off their last bits of energy. Can he use the mass confusion to his advantage?

He is just about to leave his hiding spot and move through the bushes down the slope when the unexpected happens. The girl breaks off from her group and begins moving in his direction alone.

He can scarcely believe his luck. She is making it almost too simple for him.

A wave of paranoia roils his stomach as he sweeps his lenses over the main building and the swarm of campers and counselors to make sure no has seen the girl leave. He wonders if it's a trap, if the police are filling the tree line opposite waiting for him, but when he scans the area with his field glasses he spots no sign of such a thing.

The old man fingers the satchel at his feet with the syringe and rope inside. He zooms in once more on the girl. She is eight years old, he remembers, doesn't seem to be in much of a hurry, pretty dark hair and skinny legs. Dipping in and out of his view, she begins tossing stones as she walks.

His patience has been rewarded. He reaches down for his bag. Just a few moments more and she'll be close enough for him to make his move.

One

When you know you are dying, the world shifts into a pastel phase. All the tastes, sights, smells, and sounds of this life grow dull, washing like detritus onto some bone cold beach.

That's how I have always imagined it, at least.

Now that I am actually closing in on the end I realize I need a new set of suppositions.

Tears fill my eyes at the sight of a hummingbird outside. The toast and honey I washed down with my afternoon coffee never tasted so sweet. From somewhere down the block, I hear the music of a baby's cry, and even the roaring assault of my neighbor's leaf blower rings of an orderly and benevolent domesticity. Nothing bad should ever happen when you are feeling and—maybe for the first time—really seeing such things.

Lori sits with me in the waning heat of the day, her gaze straying out the bedroom window at the rose bushes her mother used to tend. The light plays tricks with her cheeks. Still pretty, but I can't help but notice the first signs of wrinkles around her eyes—shadows of things to come. The air smells of the lingering traces of Lori's unidentifiable perfume. Her chair creaks as she kicks off her shoes and stretches her feet, legs suspended in midair.

"What did you eat for lunch today, Dad?"

She must have a million better things to do than hang around here with her old man.

"I'm sorry, what did you say?"

"You heard me."

"Would you believe beet, string bean, and cauliflower soufflé?"

"Hardly."

I smile, focusing on the quilt over my legs, double wedding ring pattern, one of Rebecca's many family heirlooms. Perched on the edge of the dresser, my antiquated television plays on low volume next to a bottle of pills. "Guess I'm not the only keen- eyed detective in the room."

"And getting more keen-eyed by the day. You've been eating more of that leftover pizza, haven't you?" Her gaze bores into mine.

"Pizza? What pizza?"

"Da-ad...You know there's way too much sodium in that crap."

"Sodium, schmodium." I used to be much better at playing this game when I was a cop.

"You've got to start keeping a closer eye on your food intake."

"You sound like some nutritional brochure."

"You know what I mean." Her voice grows quiet as she adjusts her skirt, picks up a paperback book from the bedside table.

She works at the public library now. Books have become her thing. She needs more time to get used to my unavoidable passing. To lose your last remaining parent is no easy thing.

"Whew." Lori fans the side of her face with the book. "It's hot in here. How do you stand it?"

"I don't know." I shrug. "It's not so bad."

She must wonder if my brain is deteriorating too. A

stubborn old farm boy who grew up minus the comfort of cool inside air, I've taken to turning off the house air-conditioning and throwing open the windows all day to better appreciate the distant hum of traffic floating through my Richmond West End neighborhood. Lying in wait for the tail of the occasional breeze, the smell of newly mown lawns. Lori starts to snicker, but catches herself in mid-sentence as if she needs to stifle any hint of cynical inevitability, the divided coda at which we seem to have arrived in our relationship.

"You have another doctor's appointment the day after tomorrow, remember," she says.

"I know. You don't need to remind me." I glance over her shoulder at the fading display of get-well cards on my dresser. A gift from some of my criminal justice students at VCU, it looks like it's suffering from some kind of time warp.

Lori's gaze wanders toward the open window again.

"Something is bothering you," I say.

"What?"

"Something has you worried, I can tell."

"No, Dad, I—"

"C'mon. Spill it."

She manages a tired half-smile but says nothing.

"You and Alex have another blowup?"

Alex, the father of my two grandchildren, has a law degree from the University of Virginia and a lucrative practice defending well-to-do criminals to show for it. He and Lori have been married for nearly eighteen years but are "presently estranged," as the polite like to put it. A couple of months ago Alex moved by himself into a fancy new condo downtown.

I began my career years ago with a modicum of respect for criminal lawyers and all they go through to earn their education, not to mention uphold their end of the legal justice system. But that opinion has eroded over time. Alex hasn't exactly been a boon for the lawyerly cause.

"No, Alex isn't the problem," Lori says. "Not right now at least." She hesitates, glances down at her hands. "I think I'm a failure as a mother."

"What? What would make you say that?"

She shakes her head again and pulls her hand away.

"You're not a failure," I tell her. "You're one of the best mothers I've ever known."

It's Lori who has cooked breakfast for her two kids every morning for the past seventeen years, Lori who packs the school lunches, writes out the cards and wraps the birthday presents, fills out the school forms, shows up at the games and recitals and PTA meetings. She may not be the most organized person in the world, but I've watched her for years, and I know about the compromises she's made. She has her mother's heart. She has her mother's eyes.

"Is Marnee okay?"

Barney Marnee, as her older brother Colin still likes to call her. Eight going on nine years old, and not so little anymore. I still hang onto this image of Marnee when she was a toddler, jumping out of Alex and Lori's car after it has pulled into the driveway, skipping down my walkway breathless with excitement—and I, rock-bound by an inability to show emotion, not knowing which way to turn until Marnee rushes into my arms. Something catapults time in that moment, pushing it to a spectacular radiance, like dancing, or make-believe kisses on the moon.

"Marnee's fine," Lori says. "The problem is Colin."

"Oh..." I nod as if I really know anything anymore about teenagers. "Colin again."

Lori's wireless phone burbles from inside her suit coat. She reaches for it on reflex.

I've grown to despise the things. They intrude on life far too much for my liking. Lori stares at the display.

"It's Colin. He's supposed to be picking up Marnee at her day camp out in Chesterfield." Looking annoyed, she pushes a button and welds the device to her ear. "Colin? Where are you?" She listens for a second. "You were late again? I keep telling you how important it is to be there on—"

She listens some more.

"What?" Her voice grows louder, registering anger mixed with something else, maybe fear.

I feel the need to move. I'm no invalid. Not yet, at least. I sit up and swing my legs off the bed.

The conversation goes on:

"What are you talking about?" Lori asks. More listening. "I want to speak to the camp director. Put her on the phone."

Something must be wrong with Marnee. Maybe she's sick or something. From the look on Lori's face, it isn't good. Lori slips her feet back into her shoes and, fumbling for her keys in her pocket, stands from her chair. "This can't be happening...not now," she mumbles. She smoothes the side of her suit jacket.

Memories stir in me, cases and concerns long past. When Lori gets the director on the line, she proceeds to interrogate the woman about Marnee. Listens again. "Do you even know what is happening with the children under your care?"

I can make out the director's garbled female voice speaking into Lori's ear, but little else.

"No. Listen, I want you to go find her right now. Do you understand? She must be someplace. I'm coming over there." She disconnects the phone.

"What's going on?"

"I don't know yet."

"What do you mean?"

"They can't find Marnee at her camp."

Two

Hidden beneath a false bottom in one of the dresser drawers across from my bed, lies a thick sheaf of papers I have shown to no one—curled pages torn from a yellow legal pad filled with my handwriting and bound together with a rubber band. I've been wondering if I should just go ahead and destroy the manuscript. Glancing at the top of the dresser, my thoughts race back to it now:

The Blue Hallelujah
A Memoir
By Jerry Strickland

The investigation that sent my wife Rebecca to prison started with fish. A lone fisherman on the James, at any rate, who caught more than he bargained for among the Belle Isle rocks: the partially decomposed body of a semi-nude young woman draped around a submerged log in sight of the Robert E. Lee Memorial Bridge.

The year was nineteen eighty-six. In the annals of homicide enquiries, no doubt many victims have been discovered in more exotic and colorful poses than Jacqueline Ann "Jackie" Brentlou. But the Brentlou girl was only thirteen. She was from a stable, middle-class family in Woodland Heights, the youngest of three children, and she had disappeared one beautiful spring day while walking home from school.

That made her killing far from typical of the murders my partner, Edgar Michael, and I were working in Richmond at the time. Our typical caseload consisted of gang and drug-related murders, drive-bys involving out-of-town players who plied the I-95 corridor from Miami to New York trafficking heroin or cocaine.

Officially, that didn't make the Brentlou case more of a priority than any other. Unofficially, everyone involved, from the scene techs to the office of the Chief Medical Examiner, wanted in the worst way to find whoever was responsible killing Jackie Brentlou.

And find the killer Edgar and I did, if only too late. His name was Jacob Gramm and he had raped and murdered before. Rebecca was never able to tell the whole truth about how or why she came to know about and kill Gramm. Had she done so, she might have avoided spending the last six years of her life at the Virginia Correctional Center for Women.

During his summation at Rebecca's trial, the Commonwealth's attorney chose to gloss over Gramm's guilt. Instead, he had a lot to say about vigilantism and Rebecca's state of mind. It's only fitting then that I rise here at the end of my days to set the record straight. If he knew what I knew, even that Commonwealth's attorney would have to agree. Few have ever stood as falsely accused as my Rebecca...

• • •

"What?" I glance into the bedside mirror, trying to process the impact of Lori's words. I see an old person there: same eyes and ears and nose I've always had, but face sagging, skin unraveling, hair, what small amount is left of it, disheveled.

"Her counselor thinks she may have gotten into a car with a parent of one of the other girls." Lori's voice wavers somewhere between panic and annoyance.

"Would Marnee have just up and left with someone else like that on her own?"

"No. I mean, I don't know. Colin was late again. The second time this week. It's the one thing I ask him to do in the afternoon after he finishes working at the pool."

"What's the name of the camp?"

"Camp Mohegan."

"What did the director say?"

"She sounded clueless. Some kind of mix-up, she claimed."

Hopefully, that's all it is. But Lori's concern triggers something in me. I push to my feet, ignoring a momentary vertigo, find my shoes beside the bed and work my feet into them. The room spins for a moment, but I close my eyes and wait for it to pass.

"Dad? Are you all right?"

"I'm fine." I open my eyes and reach for my wallet on the bedside table.

"Why are you standing?"

"I'm coming with you."

"Oh, no you're not. You can't. I mean, what for?"

"To help."

Our eyes meet again for a moment, some silent fear communicated between us. The walls seem to breathe in and out while my head clears. I push away from the bed, taking a couple of steps.

"You're not well," Lori says. She reaches to try to prevent me from continuing, but I shake her off.

"I'm coming, I tell you."

"But Dad—"

"Don't worry. I'm well enough."

• • •

Fifteen minutes later, we crawl in commuter traffic on the Powhite. Still a couple of miles from Camp Mohegan, Lori says. She is growing more anxious by the moment. Me too. Maybe there is an accident somewhere up ahead. The long line of brake lights in front of us would be exasperating even on a normal day.

More people live in Chesterfield now, southeast of
Richmond, than in the city itself. The county has become
one of the more prosperous portions of the urban ring, a
mostly characterless suburban homogeny that could have
just as easily sprung from Sacramento, Orlando, or Dallas,
theme park attractive yet lacking any soul.

"If I've told him once, I've told him a thousand times
'Make sure you're on time to pick up Marnee.'"

"You mean Colin."

"Who else?"

"Maybe he's got a good excuse."

"There is no excuse."

Left unspoken is the horrific possibility Marnee's
apparent disappearance might not have happened if it
weren't for Colin's tardiness. I suppose it's easier for Lori to
think about than what might be going on with Marnee.

"You said earlier there was a problem with Colin." Sad
to say, but I've been expecting trouble with my grandson.
Colin isn't a bad kid, compared with a lot I've seen. But
unlike his sister, whose bond with her mother seems to be
insulating her from the effects of the pending divorce, Colin
has taken the parental breakup like a knife to the heart. He
masks the pain the way any seventeen-year-old might, with
an I don't care attitude and occasional you can stick it where
the sun doesn't shine kind of comment that in my father's
day would have earned him a back-of-the-hand clip across
the mouth. To anyone really paying attention, the hurt leaks
out of him like an oozing wound.

Lori sighs. "You might say that."

"You catch him smoking pot again?"

"No." An errant strand of hair drops over her forehead
and she pushes it nervously away, an ancient echo from her
own long-ago childhood. She places both hands back on
the wheel.

"What then?"

"We got into an argument last night. Colin told me he wants to move in with his father."

"Oh, he did, huh?"

The news is hardly a surprise. Alex, for all his many failings, has at least made an attempt to keep up his relationship with his son.

"The kid's crafty, you've got to give him that," I say. "You keep close tabs on him, but he knows he can get away with a lot more at his father's. You think he blames you for the separation?"

"Could be." She stares aimlessly ahead.

"Maybe I should have a talk with him."

"I can't ask you to do that, Dad. I mean—"

"Why not? It's perfect, you ask me. Maybe he'll listen for a change."

She says nothing.

"Tell you what. You bring him by and the two of us will have a little chat, man to man."

"Thank you," she says. "...I don't know what else to do."

For a moment, I can't help but see her as an adolescent again herself, balanced on the precipice between innocence and worldliness, the heart-darkening knowledge that no one in this world can make everything right. I think again of her mother, wishing I could somehow reach back in time for some of Rebecca's wisdom.

"I wish all these people would just get out of our way." Lori drums her hands in frustration on the dash.

"Try turning on your hazard lights."

"That won't make any difference."

"It's worth a try."

She reaches up and turns them on. It doesn't seem to work at first, but then the car immediately in front of us switches lanes to let us pass, as do a couple of others, and soon we're making better progress.

The leather seat of Lori's Lexus feels cool against the back of my neck. I sink into it, staring out through the glass at the sea of cars and people moving in both directions. Is this our new Richmond? Bespectacled, finely-coiffed yuppies in their Izod shirts, sipping lattes or chatting and texting incessantly on their digital phones, driving their foreign SUV's to cart around their children or meet their harried co-professional wives and cheer on their progeny along the sidelines of some soccer field. I see them all the time, on the few occasions I get out anymore with Lori or someone else.

Maybe Lori has become one of them too. Maybe Marnee has simply dropped through a crack in Alex and Lori's misfiring lifestyle no one realized was there. But that's a crazy way to think, isn't it?

Lori leans on the horn and swerves around a slow-moving Chrysler driven by an elderly man probably not that much younger than myself. Looking embarrassed once she spies the driver, she plucks her cell phone from its holder on the dash.

"It's going to be okay," I say because I can think of nothing better to offer.

"I still don't believe this."

Silently I offer what I hope might pass for prayer.

"Are you sure you're all right, Dad?"

I know she worries about my heart. One of its valves is a marvel of modern engineering—it has managed to keep me going these past few years. Unfortunately, like my decrepit television, my little miracle machine is now obsolete, liable to go kaput at any time. It can't be replaced, my heart has lost most of its efficiency, and I'm no longer a transplant candidate. The last thing I want to be is another complication for Lori.

"Totally fine," I say. "Let's worry about finding Marnee."

Despite the flashers, the line of cars still seems to barely move. In frustration, Lori punches in the number on her cell phone for the cell of Candy Fletcher, the mother of Rachel Fletcher, one of Marnee's best friends. Rachel, is also attending the camp this week. She waits for the woman to answer, says hello, and they talk.

Marnee is not with them, Lori discovers. Apparently Rachel tells her mother she doesn't remember seeing Marnee in the crowd of campers when they left the camp either. Candy thought Marnee's older brother had already picked Marnee up when Rachel got in the car with her. Hardly encouraging news.

Lori disconnects the call.

"How about Alex?" I suggest. "Could he have somehow picked up Marnee by mistake?"

Lori nods, acknowledging the possibility without a word. She tries Alex's cell phone. No answer. Though it's after five, she tries calling Alex's office next. Catches Alex's secretary, who informs her Alex left work early this afternoon.

"Probably out running around with that new little friend of his," Lori mumbles to herself. "Figures."

The "friend" she refers to is a younger woman she suspects may be Alex's new ladylove, a blonde associate attorney in the midst of a marriage breakup herself. Lori fumbles with her phone again, speed dials Alex's cell number, and this time leaves a banal message wondering if by some chance he might have stopped by the camp to pick up Marnee. She hangs up in disgust.

We inch along, speeding up for a moment before slowing again. I can't think of anything else for us to do.

"Why don't you see if there is any more news from the camp?"

She nods again, searches her call screen and redials the number. Someone answers and they put the director on the phone.

I can tell from her body language the news is not good. They've asked counselors to begin scouring the camp and searching the surrounding woods; there is still no sign of Marnee. Two people are calling the cell phones of all the other parents with children at the camp today. No luck there either.

Lori's hand trembles as she places the phone back in its holder and finishes telling me about the call. "They're calling the police."

"Maybe not a bad idea. Just as a precaution." I try to sound reassuring.

With each passing minute the reality of the situation looks bleaker. Tears form around the rims of Lori's eyes, but she manages to pull it together.

"I'd offer to drive—"

"It's all right, Dad," she says. "I'll be okay."

Lori looks across at me and tries to smile. It is a gesture that speaks volumes about her character. A couple of years ago they threatened to take my driver's license away because I'm old. Part of the new more rigorous road regulations imposed on the public by those in the Virginia General Assembly under threatened sanction by Washington—politicians, statisticians, and their bureaucratic enforcers obsessed with social engineering under the guise of 'keeping the public safe.'

Why aren't they down here in Chesterfield County, Virginia at the Mohegan Day Camp helping search for a lost little girl? Why aren't they keeping her safe?

Lori's mobile rings again. She looks at the display with anticipation, obviously hoping for good news from the camp. "It's one of the other moms." She pushes the answer button with a sigh.

They talk for a minute and it immediately becomes apparent the woman has somehow gotten word about Marnee. From the look on Lori's face, it's also clear the woman has nothing substantive to offer, her motivation may be simple gossip or the macabre voyeurism that causes people to slow down to stare at traffic accidents. *I talked with her mother firsthand.*

Lori can be tough when she needs to, but somehow the woman's callousness strikes a nerve. She hangs up and almost breaks down.

"It's okay, we're going to get through this. We'll find her."

But even as the words leave my mouth they sound hollow to me, projecting confidence before we really have much of an idea of what's going on.

Lori lifts a hand off the wheel momentarily to wipe the corner of her eyes. She weaves the Lexus past a lumbering motor home.

I have an idea. "Why don't I try to reach Major Ford with the Chesterfield police? He used to go to church with your Mom. I haven't talked to him in a few years, but I think he's still head of the Investigations Bureau over there."

"You think he's at work this late?"

"Knowing Ford, he is. Or someone will know how to get hold of him."

"You know the number?"

"Not anymore. Not off the top of head."

"I'll find it." She plucks up the cell phone again and dials directory assistance.

It's good giving her something to do. She listens then hands me the phone. "The computer will automatically connect you."

I hear the line ringing and wait until a Chesterfield Police switchboard operator comes on the line. I identify myself and ask for Ford. The operator puts me on hold. All the cases and all the years I spent working the phones. The memories haunt me; I don't want to associate Marnee with any of them. Half a minute later, a voice booms through the phone.

"Jerry?"

"Yeah."

"It's Hal Ford. How in the world are you?"

"I've seen better days."

"Yeah? What's going on?"

I skip the pleasantries. Staring into the dashboard of Lori's car, I do my best to explain the situation, discussing a missing child as if she were anyone but Marnee, not doing a very good job of it, I'm afraid, out of practice as I am.

On the other end of the line, Ford's tone remains calm, professional. He asks a number of straightforward questions.

"You know she's probably just wandered off somewhere or, like you said, decided to book herself a play date with a friend," he says.

"Let's hope. But the camp director's already made the decision to call 911, so I thought I'd call you."

"Of course."

"And there's the potential complication with the father."

It's a classic story: estranged husband and wife—one spouse disappears with the child. I can't quite picture Alex fitting the mold, but we'd be foolish not to consider the possibility.

"I hear you," Ford says. He gives me his personal cell phone number and tells me he'll head to the scene himself. He asks me to call him if there are any new developments before he arrives.

"When do you, you know, make a bigger call?"

"Don't worry. If we determine there is a genuine problem, we'll immediately contact the state police to issue an Amber alert. If it comes to that, we're going to need as much information as possible."

"All right." Neither of us voices what I know he must be thinking: if Marnee's somehow gotten lost or worse, been taken by someone up to no good, the next few hours will be our best opportunity to get her back.

"Mohegan," Ford says. "I know where the place is. How soon will you be there?"

I've never been to the camp before. I glance at Lori who holds up a handful of fingers.

"My daughter says five more minutes."

"Okay," he says. "I'll be there in fifteen. And Jerry?"

"Yeah?"

"Tell your daughter not to worry. Your granddaughter, she's one of our own."

Three

Two Chesterfield County police cruisers are already on the scene when we arrive at the camp. I recognize Colin's car as well, the hand-me-down Saab his father passed on to him when Colin turned seventeen. It's parked at an odd angle in front of the camp office, which is nothing more than an air-conditioned Quonset hut with glass windows and an oversized sign above the door that reads WELCOME TO MOHEGAN. WHERE DAYS ARE ALWAYS BRIGHT.

By now, the campers have all left for the day. A small group of teens clad in yellow T-shirts, counselors apparently, huddle in front of the office talking with a couple of uniformed officers. Uphill through the trees, others can be heard searching the woods. Yet a third group of camp workers are hanging back on the periphery, curious but apparently waiting to be told what to do.

The sun beats down mercilessly here, not like the shady protection of the old growth trees around my house. As Lori and I step toward the office, one of the officers, a black woman with empathetic eyes, turns and looks our way. She seems to sense who we are. Lori breaks into a trot as we near the group in front of the building.

"I'm Mrs. Butler. Have you found my daughter?"

The counselors all stare in silence. The officer separates herself from the young people.

"They're waiting for you inside, Mrs. Butler. Right this way."

My spirit sinks. I've seen this kind of demeanor before, remember learning to display it myself. People think it's hard trying to catch a killer, and it is, but that's not what's really hard. I knew guys that would rather take a bullet than have to sit and talk with a victim's mother.

Lori reaches back to take my hand. I grasp her fingers for a moment and then we separate and are walking on either side of the officer toward the Quonset hut. The officer steers us along a narrow back walkway, leading us around front toward the main door of the building.

"This is my father Jerry. He's retired from the Richmond PD." Lori's voice sounds as if she's choking on her words, the whole scene becoming surreal.

"Yes, ma'am. Major Ford has already spoken with us. He'll be here shortly with the other detectives."

The office has a white storm door with one of those tubular, pneumatic closers and no screen but a plate of glass. Around the side of the building, a window air-conditioner hums at full blast. Through the door, I see Colin, all strapping six-foot two of him, and a blonde-haired woman about Lori's age standing in front of a desk talking with another patrol officer.

We meet a wall of cool air as we push inside. Colin catches sight of us; his face is drawn and closed. Lori glares at him for a moment before turning to the others.

"Mrs. Butler is here," the patrol officer announces before heading back out the door.

"Mrs. Butler?" The officer talking to Colin and the woman looks up. "I'm Officer Parrish."

"And I'm Jeanne Harwell, the camp director," the blonde woman says, stepping forward to shake Lori's hand. She is solidly built, athletic. She looks like she's used to being in charge. "I believe we met last week at orientation."

Lori takes the woman's hand before releasing it. "Yes, I remember," she says. "Please, somebody tell us what's going on."

"I'm so sorry. There's still no sign of Marnee." The director's eyes search ours, an ashen expression across her face bordering on dread. "But we're looking everywhere."

"I talked to the parent of her two best friends on the way over here. She's not with either of them."

"We know. As I mentioned to you on the phone, we've been calling down the list of numbers for each of the parents who had children at the camp today," the director says. "Nothing so far, but we're still waiting for some of them to call us back."

"Have you tried searching the bathrooms?"

"Yes, and turned the rest of the camp upside down as well."

Lori stares at the woman. "How could this happen?"

"We had overflow numbers today. The kids were playing a game of capture the flag. Somehow Marnee got separated from the group she was with and, well, we're not really sure what happened after that. We're questioning all the counselors. We have good security here. There's never been any problem. As I told you on the phone, the counselors from the group she was with today thought she left with another parent." Her voice, shaking, trails off.

I almost feel sorry for her. She looks competent enough, like a person overcome by events beyond her understanding.

"How many parents are there altogether?"

"Close to a hundred."

"Oh, God. This is some kind of nightmare." Lori turns to look at Colin. "Why couldn't you have gotten here on time for once?"

Colin holds out his hands. "I'm sorry, Mom, I—"

I step into the mix, looking at the officer. "What's happening with the ground search?"

The officer says, "We've got wooded areas and a construction zone for a new upscale development surrounding the camp. My partner is helping some of the senior counselors search the immediate vicinity. More units are on the way."

Lori balls her fists. It' obvious she is close to a panicky rage. We both need to be doing something. "If she didn't leave with someone, she might still be close by. And if she's hurt or in trouble, she might recognize our voices. Why don't we go see if we can help look?"

Lori looks at me for a moment, her face a mixture of emotion. "What are we waiting for then? Let's go." She turns back toward the door.

The officer holds it open for us.

"Me too." Colin jumps up to follow.

Outside, the atmosphere is filled with tension. The heat and humidity feel even more oppressive than before, and through the trees searching counselors bob in and out of the brush like rampaging animals. In the back of my mind, I can't help but consider the possibility they might be trampling over a potential crime scene, but I push the thought away. Marnee might just be lost. She could have been storing up her hurt from her parents' separation and maybe that somehow triggered her to run off.

Officer Parrish moves on ahead of the group. I'm already sweating as we cross the field and run into one of the senior counselors. Crew cut. Baggy cargo shorts. The requisite camp tee and orange flip-flops that weren't exactly made for tramping around in the woods, although the young man's making a game attempt of it.

"Anything?" Parrish asks.

The counselor shakes his head. He turns toward the woods, cups his hands around his mouth, and calls out Marnee's name. Up the hillside, the voices of other counselors ring out as well.

I turn to Lori. "You said Marnee was wearing blue jean cutoffs, sneakers and socks, and a green camper T-shirt today, is that right?"

"That's right."

"What brand are the sneakers?"

"Converse."

"What color?"

"Blue."

"What color are the socks?"

"White with green piping."

"We need to pass the word to everyone to keep an eye out for anything that looks like that. Bright colors are easier to spot in the woods."

Which is partially true, but not the whole truth. What I don't tell her is children forcibly abducted by an older person will often kick their feet defensively, many times losing a shoe or sock in the process.

I turn to Officer Parrish. "Why don't we spread out, see if we can pitch in looking, too?"

"Absolutely."

Sirens can be heard in the distance. More help is on the way.

"How do we communicate?"

"I've got one other officer with a walkie-talkie out here leading the first search group. If we stay within voice range, I can communicate with him. We've got more trained searchers and a dog unit on the way, but for the time being we're the only professional eyes out here."

Lori still wears her shoes from work. She crashes into the brush anyway and cups her hands over her mouth like the counselor.

"Marnee! Marnee, can you hear me?" They wait for a few moments, but there is no answer.

Sometimes lost toddlers, scared and disoriented, will respond more readily to a mother's voice, but Marnee is no toddler. We have no idea if she is scared or disoriented or even in the vicinity anymore. We have nothing but the trees. The dank smell of the lingering heat. The sounds of the other searchers.

"Okay, let's keep looking," Parrish says.

I fan out by myself to the right. Here the going looks a little easier, less undergrowth within the forest. Lost children usually take the path of least resistance. I'm looking for Marnee, of course, but just as importantly for any telltale sign of her presence—sneaker tracks, broken branches, scraps of fabric, any evidence an eight-year-old girl might have recently passed through here. Almost like working homicide again. I shudder at the connection.

Like an apparition, Colin appears at my side. "Can I go with you?"

"Okay. Come on."

"This sucks. Marnee probably just went home with one of her friends they haven't thought about. She's probably at the girl's house playing horses and eating cookies right now."

"Maybe."

We make a fine pair. The delinquent and the old guy. A symbiotic relationship if ever there was one.

He jumps on ahead.

"Slow down."

"What?"

"I said, slow down."

"But we'll cover less ground that way."

"It's not about speed. It's about not missing anything."

"Okay." For once, Colin does as he's told. "Don't you think we would have found her by now? I mean, if she's really out here."

I say nothing, trying to stay focused on the task at hand.

He crashes on beside me, yells Marnee's name, directing

his voice into the woods like he has seen the others do. Walk. Yell. Stop to listen. Walk some more. Still no answer from the woods, no sign of Marnee.

We cross a shallow stream, more a rivulet really. Marnee is not a strong swimmer, her mother has mentioned on a couple of occasions. I'm thankful we're not near any large body of water.

"What if we don't find her?" Colin asks a few minutes later. "What if she really is missing?"

"Then we go on to the next phase. The police will kick everything into high gear and widen the net."

"Will she be on TV?"

"We'll see. Let's just take it one step at a time. The worst thing we can do is get ahead of ourselves and miss something important. Pay attention. Look everywhere and at everything. If she's out here somewhere, she might be hurt or unconscious."

He nods, his blue eyes mimicking my examination of the ground and the surrounding thickets.

"I wasn't trying to be late, you know. The traffic—"

"Colin. We don't have time for this right now."

"Okay."

We come to an incline. I've seen nothing so far to indicate Marnee's presence. The odds of finding anything significant for any one member of a search team are extremely low. Doesn't make any searcher's role less important. All the ground has to be covered.

"What are we looking for? I mean, besides Marnee herself?"

"You know what tracking is, right?"

"Yeah. I saw a special on the Discovery Channel about some dude out in Arkansas. His face was covered in green paint and they were, like, helping to train soldiers."

"Good. Well this is something like that."

It dawns on me my young lifeguard of a grandson, raised on a diet of suburbia and shopping malls with only television and the occasional foray into a backyard tent to form his view of the woods, probably has no clue how to search for someone. With his single man earring and curly black hair he's another creature from what I was at his age. Harder around the edges maybe. Softer at the core.

"Here." I tug at his arm. "Sit down on your heels beside me here for a moment."

He follows me down into a squat position, his elbows resting on his knees.

"Gum?" I pull a stick from my pocket and offer it to him.

He shakes his head.

I pop the stick in my mouth. Sugarless, watermelon. Can't get enough of the stuff. I used to be a pack-a-day smoker before I met Rebecca. Switched to Juicy Fruit for years before the dentist convinced me to change. I point away from the path we've been taking toward the floor of the forest.

"What kind of ground do you see here?"

He shrugs. "Dirt. Some rock. A bunch of old, dead leaves."

"What kind of dirt?"

"Reddish brown."

"Is it wet or dry?"

"Mostly dry."

"But we've been having a lot of rain lately, haven't we? A lot of thunderstorms."

"Yeah. So the ground's pretty soft, I guess."

"Exactly. Better conditions to pick up a sneaker print."

"Right."

I point up the hill to the path he has just made. "Now how does it look different back that way?"

"Looks like I kicked up some leaves and stuff."

"You got it. And Marnee would have done the same. See anything else?"

He looked more closely, slowly shook his head.

"How about that little sapling you just stepped on when you came back down here?"

"Yeah. I see it."

"You see how it's bent over? The wood didn't break, not completely, but some of the leaves were damaged."

"I see it."

"That's the kind of thing we're looking for. An eight-year-old girl tromping through the woods is bound to leave signs."

He nods.

"Better we take our time. Make sure we haven't missed anything. She might have even dropped something or torn a sleeve, you never know."

We inch up the hill, crunching through leaves and brush and leaning into the terrain. We begin to move like partners, searching the gathering shadows.

I think of the last time I saw Marnee. It was the weekend before when her mother brought her by the house on the way home from ice-skating. Marnee loves to ice skate at a nearby indoor rink. No budding Michele Kwan. Just for fun with her friends. I was seated at the kitchen table. Marnee took my hand and placed it in hers. "I missed you this week, Grandpa. I missed you every day."

"I missed you too, Marnee."

A bright, inquisitive child, already reading two grades ahead in school, but a part of her is still a little girl. Will she soon outgrow such remnants of innocence soon? Probably. I hope not.

"Granddad, you hear that?"

Colin's question boots me back to reality. "Hear what?"

"Someone's yelling."

We stand still, waiting. The woods are silent for a

moment. Then a faint, indecipherable voice—someone yelling—bounces over the ridge.

"I can't make out what they're saying. Can you?"

Colin cups his ear to listen. His eyes grow wide. "It's the police." His eyes grow wide. "The police are hollering for us to come. Maybe they've found Marnee."

"Or found something." I face the direction of the voice. "C'mon."

Four

I didn't believe in love at first sight until I laid eyes on Rebecca. She stood with her whimsical smile next to an older woman, surveying the crowd at the annual policeman's benefit ball while I hovered over the food table across the room.

My captain had roped me into attending as a departmental representative.

"We drew straws," the captain had said. "You've got the least seniority and yours came up short."

"Right."

By then Rebecca had graduated from Virginia Commonwealth University with a degree in music and English literature. Educated to the ways of the world, she had developed into a winsome beauty, beguiling in her own way, and had become the object of at least a couple of potential young male suitors, neither of whom, despite their good looks, or money, or charm, appeared to have met her high standards. I was hardly the best new prospect to overturn the odds.

I approached the two women and introduced myself. At thirty, barrel-chested after seven years working patrol, I had just made detective, and, at the time, knew as much about English literature as most of the riff-raff I chased after. Raised on hardscrabble farm life, where the virtues of hard work, diligence, and molten anger were parceled out in equal increments. Still up at five each day. Fifty push-ups and sit-ups to start the morning. Religious about that, at least.

"You must be the only real policeman within a mile of this place," were the first words Rebecca ever said to me.

I laughed.

"Rebecca is a singer," the woman introducing us said.

"Really. Professional?"

"Oh, no. Just an amateur, I assure you," Rebecca said. Her shy smile could have melted.

"Oh, you're too modest," the woman went on. *"She has an incredible voice. Rebecca's father is a minister."*

I'd heard of her father's church. Willow Lawn Baptist was a big stone building with imposing columns—never had any occasion to darken the door of the place myself. *"Guess that means a lowly cop like me doesn't stand much of a chance of making the dance card,"* I said.

"Not exactly," Rebecca said. *"Isn't that why we're all here?"*

Everyone else in the room seemed to disappear.

"Can you dance?" I asked.

"Can you?"

Without another word she reached out for my hand and allowed me to guide her out onto the floor. The band was playing some kind of samba and I wheeled her round and round.

"Not bad for a detective," she said.

"I try."

"No crimes to solve tonight?"

"Criminals have all assured me they're taking the night off."

Her smile seemed to promise more than I could imagine.

Ten years on the force had just about convinced me creatures like Rebecca were merely figments of romantic moviemakers' imaginations. Handle enough garbage every day and eventually you grow immune to any beauty beyond the skin deep, even beauty that passes before your very eyes. The fact I was nearly ten years her senior also allowed me, at least for a few moments, to chalk up her sweet disposition to naiveté, although I was soon to be disabused of that idea.

Soon Rebecca's parents came to take her home. If I had known then all that was to eventually come to pass in our lives, would I have done anything differently that night? Yes. I would have paid closer attention to the moment and the beauty. I would have listened more carefully to the cadence of her voice. I would have danced with her until the end.

• • •

A small platoon of counselors, their young, sober faces drenched in sweat, has gathered in a semicircle around Lori and Officer Parrish. Colin and I are among the last to join the group.

It's a quiet spot, not far but hidden from the view of the camp next door. Crushed gravel turnaround. Freshly cut road. A sizeable development. Empty quarter acre lots. A web of new streets has been carved into this side of the ridge.

The counselors look up as we approach and part way for us. Parrish, Lori, her eyes red-rimmed with tears, and another officer are bent over something lying in the dirt at the edge of the gravel. A girl's sock. White with green piping.

I place an arm around Lori's shoulder.

"It's Marnee's, isn't it?" Colin stares at the sock.

My mind begins to sift through the possibilities. The slim chance remains Marnee could still be here in these woods, lost or injured. She may have removed this sock herself for some reason, but my experience and the concern on the faces of the patrol officers tell me otherwise. Someone very recently drove a vehicle up here and parked it in the turnaround. In all likelihood, Marnee left with that same someone. Most likely taken by force.

Parrish is speaking into his walkie-talkie.

I turn to him. "We'd better clear all these people out of here before any more evidence gets trampled on, don't you think?"

"Right." The second patrolman springs into action,

herding the group together and backing us all away from the scene, instructing everyone to be careful where they step. "We haven't let anyone touch the sock," he adds defensively.

Lori rises away from me, groaning in anguish, then, looking around, spots Colin. She glares at him.

"You selfish pig." Before I realize what's happening, she leaps at him. She grabs him by the shoulders, screaming into his face and punching him in the chest and arms with her fists. "You couldn't even get here on time!"

Colin offers little resistance, covering up with his elbows and forearms and shrinking in retreat. The second officer puts a gentle but firm blocking hand on Lori's shoulder and moves in between them. Lori turns away, sinking to her knees and burying her face in her hands.

Is it Colin Lori wants to attack or Alex? Or both? This can't be happening, God. It seems too cruel, too perverse.

I step forward, bending down, and Lori falls crying into my arms, her face turning toward mine.

"Not again, Dad," she whispers. "Not like what happened with Mom."

"I know...I know."

I hold her for a minute before turning to the patrolman. "It's okay, officer. She'll be all right."

Colin stares into the circle of faces. I make eye contact with him, too.

"She'd do the same if it happened to you."

Colin nods, looking unconvinced. He glances around at the counselors. Many of them are about his age and offer him sympathetic looks.

"Detective Strickland, Major Ford would like to speak to you."

It's Parrish talking. He is holding out a cell phone. Ford has arrived at the camp office. His voice has been booming through the officers' handsets attached to their shoulders.

"I thought he was on the walkie-talkie."

"He is. But he wants to speak to you privately."

Lori raises her head from my shoulder. Colin has recovered enough to come and stand next to us. "I'm sorry, honey." Lori, more in control now, reaches out to touch his arm. "I'm so sorry."

"I know," Colin says.

They lean together in a strained embrace.

I take the phone from Parrish. "Jerry, is that you?"

"Yeah."

"You okay?"

"Not doing so well at the moment."

"We're jumping on this with everything we've got. I'm coming up the hill with a couple of detectives and the forensics unit is on its way."

"Thank you." The stinging reality of the moment leaves me lost for words.

"I just got off the phone with the state police. We need a description, pictures, and anything else your daughter and you can give us for the Amber Alert."

Five

The woods seem to grow a few shades darker.

"We're bringing in more bottles of water." Ford continues through the phone. "And I've got crisis counselors and other support on the way."

I am only half listening. The reality of the situation has begun to sink in. Marnee is genuinely missing—this isn't about some mix-up or a little girl gone off on a lark.

"You have a pastor or a priest, someone you would like us to call?"

After her father retired from preaching Rebecca started attending the mostly black Gideon Baptist out in Chesterfield, Hal Ford's church. She said she felt more spiritually connected, felt the presence of the Holy Spirit there. You can imagine how that went over with some from her father's old congregation, not to mention her parents for different reasons. Tensions in Richmond over the forced integration of schools were still raw in the seventies. Some of her father's old parishioners still clung to their old prejudices.

I haven't maintained much of a relationship with organized religion since she died.

"No thanks, Hal. There's no one I can think of right now."

"Okay. Maybe you can help us cordon off the area. Make sure none of those kids tramples over any evidence."

"Will do."

"See you in a sec."

I hand the phone back to Officer Parrish. The other patrolman has already started to roll out a length of crime scene tape.

"Let's get all these people back down to the camp office so you guys can do your work," I hear myself saying.

"Yes, sir. I'm on it." Parrish goes to speak with the counselors and begins to herd them carefully down the hill.

Lori looks at me in shock.

"Are you all right?" I ask.

She stares blankly, waves a noncommittal hand. I search around for a place where the two of us can get off our feet. A shiny new guard railing, paid for no doubt by the developer, marks the end of the road in the shade.

"C'mon. Let's sit down here for a minute."

Colin is suddenly there by our side. He helps guide his mother over to it.

There is a practiced self-assurance about him I haven't noticed before. Maybe he knows more about crime scenes than I give him credit for? Maybe he's used to slipping in and out of the grownup world, a teenage chameleon.

Everyone else is clearing out of the area so the cops can do their work. I know we should leave, too, but I am already cataloging the scene in my mind. Breaks in the surrounding woods where the bulldozers have been hard at work. LOT FOR SALE signs from various realty companies scattered across the hillside. Service breakers for underground utilities dotting the landscape like lonely sentinels. The organic smell of newly turned earth, mud wash, and loam.

I turn to look again at Marnee's sock. It seems wholly out of place here. Like a premature relic, harbinger of families moving in, outdoor games, wholesome things that can sometimes be so suddenly taken away.

Lori must imagine the worst. She has raised her hand

over her mouth as if to fend off the horror. A female officer appears, taking Lori aside, and they move to sit together a short ways down the railing. Judging from the woman's manner, she is no doubt a mother too, talking to Lori in calm, measured tones. I am unable to make out what they are saying.

I am still thinking about all these things when something catches my eye a few feet away from the sock.

"Colin."

"Yeah?"

"Help me get back over there to take a look at this." I indicate the area around the sock with my gaze.

"But I thought you said we weren't supposed to disturb anything."

"I know. I just want to have a quick peek at something."

We push off the railing and move toward the spot in question.

"What is it?"

"It might be nothing but—"

Nearing the sock again, I see my suspicion has been correct. There is something very clearly visible in the swath of red Virginia clay to one side away from the gravel: a boot print that looks like it came from the bottom of some sort of rubber gardening boot. A woman's, judging from the size of it—or a small man's. Staring down at it, a vague memory begins to dance through my thoughts, something I can't quite get a handle on.

Officer Parrish steps into view again, a roll of crime scene tape in his hand.

"I'm sorry, Detective Strickland, but my orders are to—"

"I know." I point down at the print, nearly glowing now before me it seems. "You want to make sure your techs get photos and a good cast of that."

"Yes, sir." He looks down at the ground before glancing at Colin. "Will do."

Six

*T*wo weeks after the dance, when I finally screwed up enough courage to phone and ask her out on a date, Rebecca's response was simple and to the point.

"What took you so long?"

She acted as if we were predestined to be together and she'd just been sitting around waiting for me to get on with the show.

I took her to dinner at Maxy's, an Italian restaurant that used to stand a few blocks from her father's church. We ordered the ravioli. I was surprised when Rebecca offered to join me in drinking red wine. No Baptist jokes from me, though.

A couple of days later, after taking her to see Gregory Peck in To Kill A Mockingbird, she took me home to meet her parents. I managed not to embarrass myself during a brief conversation. It was already after ten, but I had a request.

I turned to Rebecca. "Any chance I could hear you sing?"

"I don't know. It's getting late," her mother said.

"Please."

Cynthia Schwinn, a long time music teacher, relented and we all sat down in the living room next to the piano where Rebecca took out a book of music and looked it over. Then she placed the book on top of the piano and began to sing.

A cappella, her voice was clear but gentle. She carried each note as if it was a part of her. The song, an old hymn, ebbed and flowed. I never wanted it to be over.

*"What do you think?" Rebecca asked when she finished.
"I think you sound...terrific."
Her parents smiled with apparent discomfort.
They opposed our courtship, me being a cop and worse, a
homicide detective. They held no animosity toward police officers
in general and publicly and to my face they were always polite
and respectful. But it was impossible to miss the subtle sideways
glances, the shades of disappointment in their words and
expressions.
Maybe they already sensed what was happening. Maybe
they already knew it was too late. They also must have been
concerned about the fact Rebecca, though often repentant, still
clung to an unruly streak.
But the Reverend and Mrs. Schwinn could no more have
prevented our union than I could have prevented what would
one day happen as a result of our being together.
We would eventually be married and would settle into
the small but adequate West End house I still call home. I
would go on, with Rebecca's encouragement and support, to
finish my college and advanced degrees at night. Rebecca would
make our home in addition to her volunteer work. Not a very
impressive life really, if you judged by grand, cosmopolitan
standards. But there was always something different about
Rebecca, an air of mystery to this day I find nearly impossible
to describe.
Not too long into our marriage, I was to find out just how
mysterious it was.*

• • •

Chesterfield County PD has already begun to set up a
command post by the time we make it back to the camp
office. I recognize the dark-skinned figure of Major Ford,
all six-foot-five of him, standing among an assembled group
of officers, barking instructions. Into his sixties now, I would
guess, his hair gone gray, but still an imposing sight. He
wears the same uniform as his officers—hunter green with

dark trim, black, yellow, and red arm patch—except his bears an oak leaf collar insignia. Catching sight of me walking with Lori and Colin, he breaks away from his patrol people, and strides out to greet us.

"Good to see you, Jerry," he says reaching out to shake my hand.

"Hal."

"I'm sorry it's turned out this way."

"Me, too." I nod, searching for more words again, finding none.

Ford looks at Lori. "This must be your daughter."

"That's right."

Lori extends her hand to shake his. "Lori Butler." Her voice seems drained of life.

"I feel awful about having to meet you under such circumstances, Ms. Butler. But as I'm sure you understand," Ford glances at me. "We have some questions we'd like to ask you and time is critical."

"Of course," Lori says, her eyes brimming with tears. "I understand."

"And this must be Marnee's older brother."

"Yes."

Ford also shakes hands with Colin.

The Major's immediate use of Marnee's name tells me he's already taken ownership of the situation. Some cops find it easier to maintain a certain distance when interviewing victim's families—better to remain coolly objective, they reason. I never went in for such detachment myself, and apparently neither does Ford.

A minute later, we are all seated inside the air-conditioned office, our clothes sticking to our bodies, trying to make sense of our new reality. The camp office seems almost hostile now, a place that will never carry good memories again.

No one speaks. There are new plastic bottles of water

on one of the tables. I pick one up, screw off the cap, and begin to drink.

"Hot as the dickens out there today," Ford says.

"Do you think there is any possibility Marnee may still be here at the camp?" Lori asks, still holding out hope.

Ford pauses. "There's always that chance. We won't know for sure until we've thoroughly completed our ground search, but—" He shakes his head and doesn't finish his sentence.

Lori purses her lips and nods.

"I know you've already gone over some of this with the officers, but can you begin by giving us a detailed description of what Marnee was wearing when you dropped her off at the camp this morning?"

Two detectives, one male, one female, have arrived to assist Ford during this initial interview. The younger, female investigator, short and Hispanic-looking, sits with dark, sad eyes taking notes on a legal pad. Lori hesitates, maybe feeling the effects of having to conjure up another image of Marnee. How many times will she have to go through this, I wonder. She gathers herself and repeats the particulars for the detectives:

"Blue jean cutoffs, sneakers and socks, and a green camper T-shirt today."

"Anything written on the T-shirt?"

"The camp logo. Marnee wasn't crazy about wearing it, but I made her." Lori's eyes tear up again.

"I'm sorry." Ford glances up at me before looking back at Lori. "I know this must be hard. We're also going to need a recent photograph, the sooner the better."

"Here." Colin, who is seated down the table from Lori, slips a cell phone from his shorts pocket. "I've got a picture of her right here on my phone."

"I have some on mine as well," Lori adds.

"May we have your phones?" The female detective asks.

"Just for a few minutes."

Lori and Colin hand over their phones to the younger male detective who has been standing to one side. The man gathers them in his hand and leaves through the door, allowing a breath of warm air back into the room.

"We'll upload the pictures and get them posted to the system right away," Ford says. "But back to what Marnee was wearing. Did she have anything in her hair today, like a ribbon or a bow, maybe a band for a pony tail?"

"No. Lori squirms a little in her seat. "She doesn't like anything in her hair, and she doesn't like pony tails."

"You said she was wearing sneakers?" Ford is persistent.

"That's right."

"What brand?"

"Converse. And they're blue."

"Low tops or high tops?"

"Low tops."

"What size?"

"Twelve. Children's size twelve."

"What about her underwear?"

"Her underwear?"

"Yes."

Lori's face fills with exasperation and then horror as she realizes the potential implications.

"I'm sorry, Ms. Butler, but the more details we have, the better chance we have of finding Marnee."

Lori nods and bites her lip. "Well, she dresses herself now in the morning, of course. I'd have to go through her drawer at home. I'm sorry, I'm not..." She seems lost for words.

"No problem, Ms. Butler. That's fine. It's not critical at the moment."

If there is any hint about Lori being less of a mother because she doesn't know what color underwear Marnee was wearing this morning, it isn't coming from Ford. But you can read it in Lori's eyes: the awareness others might judge her, doubts that always seem to arise at moments of weakness, maybe she shouldn't be trying to balance motherhood and working outside the home.

Ford leans forward in his chair. I have been there enough times myself to know they are about to step up the questions, to move beyond the basics of pictures and clothing.

"Does Mr. Butler know Marnee is missing?" he asks.

Lori's countenance darkens. "No. I haven't been able to get through to him."

"Why not?"

"We're separated," Lori says.

Ford glances at me than looks back to Lori. "Right, that's what your father told me on the phone."

"I tried calling his office," Lori continues, "to see if by any chance he might have picked Marnee up, but his secretary said he had left early for the day, and he didn't answer his cell phone when I called."

"Did you leave a message?"

"Yes. But I didn't tell him about Marnee. I mean at the time, we didn't know…I just asked him to call me back."

Ford turns and looks over his shoulder at one of the officers. "We're going to need all of his contact information." He turns back to Lori.

"I guess you should also know I've filed for divorce," Lori says.

Ford works his jaw in a circle, a cloud passing across his face. "And the children are living with you?"

"Yes."

"Any history of violence?"

"I don't—" Lori looks confused. "What do you mean?"

"Has your husband ever hit you or the children?"

"No. Alex would never, I mean, you don't think. You don't think Alex would have—"

"I don't think anything at this point, Mrs. Butler. But we need to find your husband ASAP and inform him of what is happening. We can send a car over to his office and his place of residence. Where is he living now?"

"He's rented a condominium down near the financial district and Shockoe Bottom. I haven't been there myself." She gives him the address.

Ford looks back at Lori. "Have you discussed custody of your children with your attorney or your husband, Ms. Butler?"

"I have temporary custody," Lori says. "Alex hasn't contested it. He has visitation rights. He's an attorney himself, but—"

"Have you talked the situation through with him? Are you sure he's okay with the arrangements?"

"Well, no. I have temporary custody, as I said. But this is crazy. Alex would never—"

"Has he said anything to you about not being happy or about trying to gain custody of Marnee and Colin?"

"No, but...I did get into an argument with him once about it. Several months ago, before we separated."

This is all news to me. I guess it's not the kind of information a daughter wants to get into with her old man.

"What kind of an argument?" Ford presses the issue.

"It was crazy." Lori's face registers a mixture of memory and discomfort. "He said he and I had no more excitement between us, Marnee and Colin were the only piece of joy left to us, and if I ever left him or did anything to jeopardize his standing with them, he'd have to take legal matters into his own hands."

I can't take it any more. "That's rich."

Ford ignores me. He turns his attention on Colin again. "How about you, son? Has your father said anything to you about any of this?"

Colin sticks his hands in his pockets and glances down

at the floor for a moment before looking back at Ford. "No, but Dad would never, I mean, I've been talking to him about maybe trying to move in with him and all. I just told my mom about it last night."

Lori closes her eyes, lowers her head, and begins shaking her head.

"But he hasn't said anything about Marnee." Colin's voice rises a little. "Nothing about Marnee at all."

I hate to have to be the one to bring up evidence exonerating my future ex son-in- law, but I must.

"The sock, Hal. If she went voluntarily with her father, I don't think we'd have found the sock."

Ford nods, running a finger along the side of his face. He sits back in his chair and holds up his hands. "Okay. Let's not any of us get ahead of ourselves. We'll send the Richmond PD over to the father's residence and check on his office again. What kind of vehicle does he drive?"

"Dark green Escalade," Colin offers.

"Virginia plates?"

Colin nods. "The plates say A&L 1."

Alex & Lori

I wonder why Alex hasn't changed the plates on his SUV. Probably just hasn't gotten around to it. The idea Alex might have something to do with Marnee's disappearance stirs up visions of manipulation and coercion. Taking off with his own daughter doesn't seem like Alex's style. I suppose it might just be possible she slipped off her socks for some reason, to change into sandals he had brought perhaps, and one of them may have dropped to the ground as she was climbing into her father's car, but it's a long shot.

Lori raises her head and opens her eyes. "I want you to take me to his condo."

Ford glances at me again before looking back at Lori. "I'm sorry, ma'am, you want to, what?"

"I said, I want to go to my husband's condo. Now. If

there's even the slightest chance he's taken Marnee, I want
to go there."

"Ma'am, we're already putting out an Amber Alert and
people are combing the area where the sock was found."

I try to intervene. "Lori, I don't think—"

"No, Dad. You don't know Alex the way I do. He's
always kept things from me, especially about his work and
money and other things. He's keeping things from me now.
I can't believe he'd take Marnee, but to tell the truth, I'm
no longer sure what he might be capable of."

"No way," Colin interrupts our exchange.

"I'm not saying he's planning to hurt her, Colin." Lori
swivels her steely gaze on my grandson, who falls silent.

Ford looks uncertain. He obviously finds himself in
an awkward position. Knowing what Lori has asked for is
unwise, potentially dangerous even, but wanting to be seen
as accommodating to the daughter of a fellow cop, he turns
to look at me. "What do you think, Jerry?"

Lori hasn't exactly had the easiest of times in life. From
the time she became an adult, and especially after she began
having children of her own, I have known better than to
try to micromanage her concerns. I can no more talk her
out of anything than I can magically produce the missing
Marnee at the moment.

"As long as you keep the situation under control, I
don't see what harm it can do," I say.

"All right. Then you and your grandson can come, too.
We can all go together in my car."

Seven

The old man peeks out through an opening in the living room curtains. All quiet, good.

He surveys the empty street below. Most people are home from work by now, inside their conditioned homes preparing dinner or whatever to get out of the heat. The nosy neighbor who lives two houses down—a thirty-something computer programmer who seems to have appointed himself guardian of the block judging by the way he pokes himself into the old man's business—brought his trash out to the curb an hour ago, but hasn't been seen since.

The old man has the radio and television tuned to the local news with the volume turned low. He is also monitoring the police scanner he has set up in the kitchen for any information about the kidnapping and Amber Alert. Roadblocks have been set up along the major highways, he has learned. Cars are being searched. Little do they know. The public and police are all on the lookout for the girl sleeping peacefully on a mattress on the floor in one of his back bedrooms.

Except for the brief, initial struggle, he hasn't harmed the girl. Not yet, at least. All those years of administering medication as an Army corpsman have served him well. He has the child gagged and handcuffed to the pipe in case the effects of the drug wear off and she starts to wake up.

The second story apartment is the perfect place to lay low for the night. Especially since he has owned the duplex for a long time, another remnant of the time he lived and worked in the Richmond area years before. He has a contract to sell the place. His tenants have all been moved out, and no one will think it odd or out of place to see him poking around the building doing a little clean up. His sister lives not too far away as well. He still loves her as a brother, but her ever-encroaching dementia makes it hard. Yet another problem he knows he's going to have to deal with, maybe soon.

At his age and station, life shouldn't have to be this difficult.

The old man thinks about his devoted, daily-Catholic mass-attending wife Carol at home in their comfortable suburban house in Arlington outside D.C. She's probably puttering around the house with their big Irish setter Libby, watering the plants and preparing dinner with the radio tuned to her beloved Washington Nationals, the Nats playing a twin bill in Pittsburgh tonight.

She thinks he's out in their boat on the Chesapeake Bay, a fishing trip he's been planning for a couple of weeks, and doesn't expect him back until the day after tomorrow. He hopes it will be enough time to do what he needs to do.

Carol has no idea about the double life he's been leading, about the group of heavies he's in debt to, the every-other-month runs to Atlantic City he's been making for years. They've never had children of their own and have always lived a compartmentalized life together, a don't ask/don't tell of their own making, a reasonably happy couple in spite of their differences. They still have a decent lifestyle, too. But the old man worries the nest egg may be dwindling.

The Atlantic City problem (how he frames it) is still manageable. And if the second part of his plan with the girl works out, it may even go away for good.

What isn't manageable at all is the ugly window on his past the little girl sleeping in the back has cracked open. He needs to make sure the window gets slammed shut again.

• • •

Alex's apartment turns out to be an end unit in an upscale condominium complex called Point Of The James. Pock-marked by visible boulders at the height of the dry season, the river flows behind floodwalls a few dozen yards below the entrance. The city skyline glows as a backdrop in the early evening light.

Before leaving the camp, Lori left him a more detailed voice mail message about Marnee being missing. Colin sits next to me in the back seat. Lori is in the passenger seat up front across from Ford who is behind the wheel. Lori's face betrays little emotion, but I imagine she must be a little crestfallen at seeing such a tangible symbol of Alex's new life.

Ford has already cautioned Lori about staying with the car while they check the place out. The last thing he wants is some kind of confrontation, especially if Marnee is with Alex.

A cruiser from the Richmond PD is already waiting in front of the condo itself. Ford rolls down his window as one of the uniformed officer approaches.

"Looks like there's no one home, Major. No sign of any vehicle matching the description. We tried the doorbell three times."

"No sign of any activity inside?"

"Negative. Far as we can tell, the place looks dark."

"Dad gave me a key," Colin offers.

"We don't have a search warrant," Ford says.

"But you've got probable cause a child may be in danger," I remind him. I don't want to push him into going inside the condo without a warrant, but I know Lori won't be satisfied until we do. Besides, it's not like we're breaking and entering.

"All right," Ford says. "But with all due respect, Mrs. Butler, I'd like you to remain here with your father until we're sure no one is at home. Your son too, I'm afraid. Is there an alarm?"

"Yeah," Colin says. "Keypad's just inside the front door." He recites the deactivation code, produces the key from his pocket, and hands it to Ford.

"Okay, you all sit tight for a couple of minutes while we check this out," Ford says. "I'll be back for you."

Ford exits the cruiser. He says something to the assembled officers. There are four of them now, and two accompany Ford up the front steps of the condo while the others head around back.

"This is lame," Colin says. "Dad wouldn't take Marnee."

Lori looks back at him with sad eyes. "I hope you're wrong."

I understand what she means. Lori's immediate obsession with Alex is a good way of avoiding the more horrible possibility: Marnee has been taken by some stranger. Alex, at least, is the devil we know.

Memories of old cases flood my mind.

The seventeen year old twin brothers from Hanover, handsome young men, both football players, gunned down in the parking lot of a shopping mall because they stood up to some local gang bangers, one of whom was trying to get into the pants of their younger sister. The pretty, middle-aged schoolteacher from the Fan District, found in her bathtub with the water still running, nearly strangled to death before she was drowned. Dozens more like them. I push them all away.

A minute later, Ford comes bounding back down the condo steps. He hangs up his cell phone, which he's been holding to his ear, and leans in through the driver's window.

"Nobody's here. I just got off the phone with someone from the Richmond PD. They're down at Mr. Butler's office. His secretary told them Mr. Butler said he'd be taking a long weekend, that he'd be away from any phones and out of range of his cell."

"He didn't say where?" I ask.

"She told the officers she has no idea." Ford looks into the back seat. "Nothing seems to be out of order here in the condo. Colin, you want to come in and have a quick peek just to be sure?"

Up the stairs to his right, someone emerges from the neighboring condo: a middle- aged woman with dark hair in a business suit. She descends the steps and strides over to us.

"I live next door. May I ask what's happening?"

Ford looks at her. "A missing person investigation."

"Are you looking for Alex Butler?"

"That's right."

"He said he was leaving for the weekend. He asked if I would bring in his mail and his newspaper."

"Did he say where he was going?"

"He said he was headed to the beach."

"Just the beach, nothing more specific?"

"I'm sorry. No."

"He leave a phone number besides his mobile?"

She shakes her head. "I hope he's all right."

"We hope so, too, ma'am. Thank you for your help."

Lori, stone-faced, turns to look up the stairs at her soon-to-be ex-husband's new home. Ford's eyes meet mine. We can't afford too many more dead ends.

Eight

Back in the west end, my house looks just as deserted as Alex's condo. Colin and I pull into the driveway in the Saab. We've come back here to grab a quick bite to eat and to pick up my reading glasses before heading back out to the camp. Lori has remained there with Ford to help work the phones while the ground search continues and to be there as the Midlothian detectives finish questioning the camp director and all of the counselors. She seems to have rallied to the cause. Which I hope will help keep her from imagining dark things.

The sun has dropped below the treetops to the west. It will be dark in a little more than an hour. Wherever Marnee is, that can't be good.

"You should be with your mother," I tell Colin.

"It's okay, Granddad. I'd rather be here with you."

"Away from her wrath, you mean."

"Yeah. I suppose."

"She can have a temper, but she doesn't mean it."

"Whatever."

"Are you still beating yourself up about being late to pick up Marnee from the camp?"

"Wouldn't you?"

I think about it for a moment. "You're right, I would. But it's history now and neither of us can change that. The most important thing is what you do from here on in."

"Okay," he says, his voice trailing off, sounding unconvinced.

The kitchen screen door bangs shut behind us. Colin tosses my house key on the table. I sit down, he pulls out another chair from the table and sits beside me.

"You want water or something to drink?" he asks.

"Sure, thanks, and help yourself, too. I've also got some fruit juice in the door of the fridge. There should be some bread and maybe some tuna fish in there, too."

Colin jumps up and retrieves a couple of plastic tumblers from the cupboard above the sink. He pours two glassfuls of apple juice and sets one down in front of me. The cold, sweet liquid tastes good.

"I can make sandwiches," he says.

"No, thanks. Not hungry. But you get whatever you like."

"I'm not hungry either." But he takes a banana from a bowl on the counter, peels it, and begins to eat.

My mind is busy spinning with possibilities, sifting through the information we've gathered about Marnee's disappearance. Colin places his elbows on the table and runs his fingers through his purposely-disheveled dark hair. He looks shell-shocked.

"You say to stop beating myself up about it, but Mom's going to blame me forever if anything happens to Marnee."

"Maybe. Don't be so sure."

"You want to know what I was doing? Why I was late picking her up?"

"Was it something illegal?"

"No."

"That's a good start then."

"I was with a girl."

"A girl."

"That's right."

"Alone?"

"Sort of."

Not sure what he means, but I press forward.

"What's this girl's name?"

"Allison."

"What were you doing with this Allison?"

"She was going to get in trouble if I didn't give her a ride from her summer job at the pool restaurant back to her parent's house."

"And that was more important than picking up your little sister."

"I didn't think it would take me so long. There was too much traffic. Usually, if you're late, the counselors just hang out with the kids for a few extra minutes anyway. It's no big deal."

"So you've been late to pick up Marnee before."

He sighs to himself. "Once or twice."

Which probably means a number of times.

"How do you think that makes Marnee feel?"

"She gets mad. Especially since Dad moved out, she always wants me to be right on time."

"You think she'd ever be mad enough to do something about it?"

"What do you mean?"

"Would she ever leave with somebody else? Take off, just to get back at you."

"No. I mean, I don't know." He shrugs. "I guess it could happen."

Now is not the time to lecture. Colin seems as frantic as any of us about finding Marnee, which may just come in handy with what I'm needing him to do now. Something's been bothering me ever since we found Marnee's sock out at the camp. Something about the boot print we saw.

"C'mon." I push to my feet. "I want to show you something."

He follows me out of the kitchen and across the dining

room floor. But instead of turning toward my bedroom, where my fatigue has me spending more and more time these days, I head toward the cellar door.

"Where are we going?"

"Down to the basement."

"Can you manage the stairs okay?"

I give him a withering glance. "How many years have I lived in this house?"

"Okay. But why don't I go first?"

I hate being treated like a child. "Suit yourself."

He starts to move through the open door.

"You know where the light switch is?"

"Not really. I think I was only down here once before." He has already descended a step or two.

"You can find it right there on the wall to your left."

"Got it." He flips the switch and the wooden stairwell is bathed with light from below.

There is nothing unusual about the descent into my basement. It's just a middle class, subterranean, finished floor. I spruced it up a bit a few years back, added a fresh coat of paint to the paneled walls and some recessed lighting. The air smells a little musty these days. I only make it down here a couple of times a week to empty the dehumidifier.

At the bottom of the stairs, I survey the recreation room, which contains a makeshift bar (unstocked these days), a dated television, a card table, and several board games stacked along a shelf. A hallway to the left leads to a pair of closed doors.

"What are we doing down here?"

"Going to my old home office."

"For your teaching?"

"No. The spare bedroom upstairs has a desk where I do most of my teaching-related work. I'm talking about the room I used back when I was a detective."

Another door at the end of the hallway stands closed

and locked. There is a layer of dust along the baseboard and the paint has faded. Lori's the only other person, besides Rebecca, who has ever been in my office, and then only to clean a couple of times since her mother's death. I haven't been inside myself for nearly a year.

The hallway ends in a storage area filled with old boxes I've never gotten around to sorting. I brace myself against the wall and point toward the opposite end of the hall.

"There's a key over there. It's on a small hook, hanging behind the hot water heater."

Colin trots over and retrieves the key while I make my way down to the office.

"That's it. Good boy. Now let's see if we can open this door."

I insert the key into the latch, turn the handle, and the door swings open. Colin moves next to me and we take a look through. The office is windowless and dark, reeking of stale humidity and years.

"Light switch is just inside."

He reaches around, flicks it on, and the room fills with a soft fluorescent glow. The light reveals a decent-sized space containing a couple of small desks, a large filing cabinet, a long wooden table and several shelves lined with cardboard boxes. Colin steps to one side to allow me to enter.

"You've never been down here before, have you?"

"No, sir."

"It's not a place for visitors."

The file boxes I've brought him down here to see are stacked two high on the table. They run almost the length of the room. But they're not what captures Colin's attention. A bulletin board hangs on one wall, its contents dusty and showing their age.

"What are all these?" he asks.

They are photos. Dozens upon dozens of old snapshots of people. Young and old, black, white, or Latino, male and female.

"Pictures of dead folks," I say.

His eyes grow wider. We walk over to examine the display.

"These are all the cases I worked on over the years."

He stares soberly at the faces.

Looking at the board is like looking at a personal history of murder in the city of Richmond—from the usual variety of urban killings to the disproportionate number of black faces related to the gang and drug murders of the eighties and early nineties. And Edgar and I didn't even work all of the cases. I can't help thinking about Rebecca, who spent so much time down here with me.

"Did you catch the people who killed everyone in these pictures, Granddad?"

"Not all of them. I wish we did."

"But you did pretty good, right?"

"We did all right."

"You trying to scare me bringing me down here?"

"Scare you? No."

He runs his fingers through his long black hair. "But what if anything bad happened to Marnee?"

"Look." I place a hand on his shoulder. "Things can happen in life. Like what happened to these people in the photos. We can't always explain them. That doesn't mean we should go jumping to conclusions about Marnee."

"Yeah. Sure." He doesn't sound convinced.

A pair of identical office chairs faces a small desk in the corner below the bulletin board. Colin wheels them over for us to sit in.

"I don't know if I should be down here."

"It's all right. We need to look through these files."

He pauses for a moment, glancing from me back to the bulletin board. "Okay."

I pick up a pencil lying on the desk and use it to point at the row of boxes. "You see all these old case files I've kept?"

"Yeah."

"And those pictures up there on the board?"

"Yeah."

"They're copies. The originals are all downtown."

"Sure."

"Let's get started then. I'm looking for something in particular."

Nine

A month after we started dating Rebecca told me how she had been raped.

"You know the old stereotype about preachers' kids," she said. "Well I was a loose cannon all right. Until something happened."

Growing up, Rebecca attended Huguenot High School in the city. When she was about fifteen, she met and befriended a student named Carlita Jimenez. Carlita, like Rebecca, was a vivacious girl and the two of them hit if off like sisters. Carlita earned decent grades in school and was, also like Rebecca, preparing to go to college. But they liked to party, too, and both liked to drink. Carlita was one of six children. Her father was a Postal worker in the city and her mother was a seamstress.

Carlita and Rebecca helped produce the school newspaper. One winter night when they were on their way home together from a weekly newspaper meeting they were met by Carlita's older cousin Tito, a weightlifter who spent hours in the gym. Tito had scored a six-pack of beer and a bottle of tequila from the storeroom of his father's store. He asked the girls if they wanted to hang out with him. They were game.

Tito then took them into an abandoned building where they all drank for a while. But then something snapped in Carlita's cousin. He pulled out a knife. He tied up both girls and raped each of them repeatedly.

Somehow Carlita was able to break free of the rope Tito

had used to bind them. She fought with Tito and screamed at Rebecca to run. Rebecca managed to stumble her way back out onto the street where a passerby called police. When they arrived a few minutes later, Carlita and Tito were nowhere to be found, but there was blood on the floor and a rope just as Rebecca had described. Carlita's body was discovered early the next morning, stuffed into a garbage dumpster behind a restaurant a few blocks from where she lived.

The murder made all the headlines and was prominently featured on the TV news, although because the girls were minors and to protect Rebecca's family's privacy, Rebecca's name was never made public. Tito was eventually arrested. Rebecca had to testify at his trial, which only made things worse. He was convicted and sentenced to spend most of the rest of his life in prison.

Rebecca's hands trembled a little as she finished telling me her story. I folded them in mine and held onto them. Her fingers were cool to the touch.

"You must see this kind of thing all the time," she said. "Doing what you do."

"Never makes it any easier. The day it does I'll quit."

She nodded.

After Carlita was murdered her mother gave Rebecca a note with one of Carlita's prize possessions, a bracelet Carlita often wore. A couple of years after Rebecca passed, I finally got up the gumption to clean out her closet. There among the necklaces, earrings, and rings arrayed in her jewelry box, I found the note and Carlita Jimenez's charm bracelet. Though I had never seen Rebecca wear it, she had always kept it close.

I tried not to think too much about what had happened to Rebecca and Carlita. It caused a blood anger to swell up in me I found difficult to control. But I also knew what her rapist had unleashed in Rebecca: a virtual certainty, if she had anything to say about it, he and all those like him would be hunted down.

• • •

Colin glances at the wall of the dead again. "I guess there's a lot of bad stuff to look at down here then."

"Yes, there is. And you're going to have to help me sift through some of it."

"Me?"

"You."

"All right. I guess that's cool."

"Remember those boot prints we saw back out at the camp?"

"Sure."

"They looked awfully familiar. And now I think I remember where I may have seen ones like them before. It was from one of these cases in the files here."

"What case? When?"

"Jackie Brentlou."

"Wait a minute. Wasn't she the one who—?"

"That's right. She was the girl murdered by the man your grandmother was convicted of killing."

He looks at me as if I've blown a gasket. "Man, that's just too weird."

"I know it sounds crazy. But I'm pretty sure I remember seeing footprints just like the ones we saw this afternoon in connection to that case."

It sounds so outlandish; I'm almost tempted to dismiss it out of hand. But as I sit among the boxes and the pictures on the wall next to my rickety old home office desk and think back to all the times Rebecca and I worked together down here, I can't help but feel as if I'm on to something.

"You find the box for the Brentlou case?"

"It's right here." He slides a carton with "Brentlou, 1986" written in bold magic marker on the top in front of me on the table. To our left sits a bookshelf lined with similar boxes, all arranged in neat chronological order.

"Strange. I don't remember taking this one out."

"Maybe you just forgot."

"Maybe."

The handwriting on the label is Rebecca's. Her neat cursive, always legible, with no room for doubt. Rebecca helped keep me organized and often labeled my files.

Colin lifts the top off.

Inside is the initial report Edgar and I wrote, along with a thick stack of evidence files, reports, and witness affidavits. Sparks dance along my spine as I remember Rebecca praying with me over some of these very scraps of paper, then, afterward, the determined effort to track down Jacob Gramm. What drove us through all those years, I wonder. Was it faith or our own form of pride? The fine and bitter determination with all that could go wrong with the world, here was something that made sense, something we could try to make right.

Some of the sections of the file are out of order and some of the papers are askew. I rifle through them in search of the footprint photos and documentation I remember.

"You know what you're looking for, Granddad?"

"I do."

And, of course, here it is in my hand. I stare at the photo. The never explained footprints discovered at the Smith crime scene were of a woman's gardening boot, size seven and a half. The mother of the dead girl didn't own such a pair of footwear. The footprints in the photo look identical to the ones we saw a couple of hours ago, but there is no name or identifying marker attached to photo, just the picture itself.

"Are they the same?" Colin peeks over my shoulder.

"Maybe. But it's crazy. Maybe it's just some kind of bizarre coincidence."

I'm trying to connect all the dots from twenty years before. But something is still missing, something just out of reach of my memory.

"Colin?"

"Yeah?"

"You ever forget stuff sometimes?"

"Sure."

"You ever talk to someone else to try to get them to help you remember?"

"Sometimes, I guess."

I place the photos back in the file for safekeeping. "Get your car keys. We need to go back out."

Ten

*T*he April rains fell in abundance that spring, soaking the
lawns and streets of the city and raising hopes for a
temperate summer. We returned home from dinner late one
Saturday night, me full of amorous intentions envisioning an
evening spent by the fire with Rebecca and a bottle of wine,
when my pager went off.

"Crap."

The readout on the display was from dispatch. I had meant
to turn the thing off, at least for a while.

"It's okay. Go ahead and answer it."

I sighed and shook my head. "Always happens."

"Not always." She reached for my hands and pulled me
into an embrace, kissing me gently on the lips. "It's all right. I
can wait. Go ahead."

The call-out was to a vacant lot in Montrose Heights where
Edgar and I would spend the next three hours.

As it turned out, the victim's name was Marshall Trane, a
twenty-four-year-old shipping clerk who'd last been seen the
night before leaving the downtown restaurant where his fiancé
worked as a waitress. It had been the fiancé who found the
blood on the handle of Trane's car door, parked, where he often
left it, in front of her apartment in the Fan.

I didn't make it home that night until after two a.m.,
bone weary, my mind a haze of frustration and fatigue. I was
barely into my thirties and already feeling too old for homicide.

Tonight was supposed to have been a complete night off for Edgar and me, a time to float serenely home, in my case, or, as in Edgar's, to the nearest eating establishment with a bar, in order to escape the hard pavement of work and bask in the balmy currents of whatever kind of tranquility, be it booze or wife, we might be able to arrange for ourselves. Rebecca had seen me work late cases before, but I knew it didn't make it any easier. A new bride deserved better.

Creeping into the quiet of our bedroom, I tried making as little noise as possible. The room smelled sweet with Rebecca's sleep, the curve of her leg lying motionless beneath the covers beside the gentle rise and fall of her breathing. I gingerly emptied the change from my pockets and placed my wallet and badge in the bedside drawer next to my gun.

I thought Rebecca was still slumbering, but she suddenly lifted her head full of curls and opened her eyes to take me in.

"Hey, stranger."

"Hey. I thought you were sleeping." I bent over to brush her lips with mine.

She smiled. "How'd it go?"

"Rough."

"Mmmmmmmm."

I said nothing more. No sense encouraging her. By now you would've thought we'd have been beyond all that, and to tell you the truth, despite the lateness of the hour and the hollow feeling wracking my bones, I was, at the furthest reaches of my imagination, a little curious about what she might have to say. But nothing prepared me for what happened next.

Rebecca lifted the sheets and kissed me harder on the lips before laying down again on her side with her back to me. I spooned in behind her, wrapping an arm around her waist and burying my face in the back of her neck.

"You make an identification yet?" She stirred, molding her body into mine.

"What?" I wasn't sure I'd heard what she said.

"Did you identify the body yet?"

The last thing I felt like talking about was the case. The sounds of the wind and the rain outside went from stark and depressing to something almost soothing, the faint coconut smell from Rebecca's washed hair reminding me there were cleaner things in the world, thankfully, than broken bodies buried among splintered wood and refuse. I wanted Rebecca to provide escape, not consultation, so I pretended I didn't heard her.

But Rebecca wasn't about to be fooled. She waited me out.

"It's a young guy. A teacher," I finally said.

"How awful."

"Yes." I closed my eyes and kissed her bare shoulder, hoping that would be the end of it.

"Did you find anything helpful at the scene?"

"What?" I opened my eyes again.

"Did you find anything useful at the scene?"

The old Bulova timepiece on our dresser, an heirloom from her mother, ticked away in the quiet. "Do you really want to get into this right now, honey? I mean, it's late, and we're both tired and—"

"I do."

"Why?"

Rebecca gently pried herself from my arms, turned over to face me, and wrapped her slender fingers around the back of my neck. "Jerry, I have something to tell you," she said.

• • •

My old partner Edgar Michael's only child, a son named Harold, died in an automobile accident a decade ago. Between periods of lucidity, Edgar sometimes can't recall the accident happened or even who Harold was. His grandchildren have shelved Edgar in a brick and columned edifice known as Royal Manor, a loosely named tribute to nobility wrapped up in the form of a nursing home that, like its occupants, has begun to go to seed.

I used to visit Edgar every Wednesday, but I haven't been by to see him in some time. So the young gal at the front desk is taken aback to see me amble through the front door with Colin by my side. Darkness has fallen outside.

"Mr. Strickland. What a nice surprise."

The girl's name is Jessica, though she goes by Jesse. She's a cute young thing, in a punk-rock, nose-ring, haven't-decided-whether-or-not-to-grow-up-yet sort of way. Most times, I flirt with her for a minute or two before going in to see Edgar, but not today.

"Need to see Edgar, pronto."

"Sure, okay." She raises an eyebrow. "I think he's down in the TV room with a couple of the other residents."

'Residents' is the euphemistic phrase the facility uses for their permanent patients. It seems to work well, most of the time, for Edgar. That is, when he's not griping about the food or the temperature in his room or the malodorous air usually wafting through the place.

Colin already looks enamored of Jessica.

"You mind?" I ask, turning down the hall in the direction of the TV lounge.

"No. No, of course not," she says.

"C'mon, Colin," I say over my shoulder. "Oh, by the way, Jessica, this is my grandson."

"Nice to meet you, Colin." Jessica says, her voice falling away at my back.

"Nice to meet you, too."

Picking up steam, I'm already three strides past the reception desk. Colin, has to rush to catch up.

"You seem to know your way around here pretty well," he says.

"Like I told you, Edgar and I go way back. More than that, actually."

I don't elaborate and Colin doesn't ask. Why should he care on a cold December night thirty years ago Edgar

Michael saved my life by scooping my wounded butt off the pavement before a partially handcuffed, knife wielding suspect could finish the job? I didn't miss much back in those days, but I'd missed that blade. And that, Edgar said, was why you never went into a situation without backup. It was all he said about the incident, and he never brought it up again.

The TV room is down at the end of the hall, a converted sun porch with beveled glass French doors and heavy curtains trimmed with lace. Three men sit tortoise-like around a credenza with a television console perched on top. Two of the men are in wheelchairs and the third one, seated on the end of a long couch, wears an oversized hearing aid. One of the men in the wheelchairs is Edgar, his chest shrunk smaller than his waist, the sides of his skull seemingly pushed in as well, bobbing the white hair on his head at the TV.

"Jerry." He looks up at us in alarm as we enter the room. "Holy Mackerel, Jerry, did you see this?"

His bony finger is pointing at the TV where a solemn news announcer is reading from a piece of paper with a photograph of Marnee highlighted in the corner of the screen and bold dark letters on a yellow background ticker taping across the bottom of the picture reading AMBER ALERT.

"That's why I'm here, Edgar."

"That's. That's." He stumbles over his words.

You should know Edgar, in his prime, was a dark-haired bull of a man, who took no guff from anyone, whether it be a suspect or any of the RPD's more bureaucratic types downtown.

Now, he's been reduced to the dependence of a child. A thin string of saliva wisps from the corner of his mouth and drops onto the front of the sweater he is wearing. He is oblivious to it. But the fire in his eyes looking at the TV screen tells me there's still a good deal of the old Edgar left.

"You remember Marnee, don't you?"

"That's your granddaughter."

"That's right."

I stand beside his chair and Colin squats down beside him to get a better look at what they're watching.

Edgar's gaze darts back and forth from Colin to the screen and then back to me. "My God, Jer, what's going on? What's happening?"

"Marnee went missing this afternoon from her camp out in Chesterfield. The police think Lori's husband, Marnee's and Colin here's dad Alex, might have taken her."

"Who's this, your grandson?"

"Yes."

Edgar nods at Colin. "And this Alex, he's the guy who's divorcing your Lori?"

"Right."

"Where'd he go with the little girl?"

"No one seems to know if he's even got her for sure. Either way, they haven't been able to find him."

"I'm sorry, Jer. Jeez, I am sorry."

Here is the thing about Edgar. Sometimes, when his memory returns, his talk and his demeanor flash blazingly bright. At other times, his thinking appears to get tangled, like too many wires clogging a circuit. I'm hoping I've caught him at one of his better interludes. I need him to try to help me remember more details about the boot prints from the Jackie Brentlou case.

"Ed, we're working on a short string here. I'm not inclined to think Alex, schmuck I think he is, took the little girl. I'm working on another theory and I need you to try to help me figure it out."

The other two men in the room have said nothing up to this point. They've simply sat staring at us like a couple of zombies from their chairs. But now the man on the couch, a short fellow with pale brown hair, looks me over.

"You a cop like Edgar here, ain't you?"

"Was," I say. "Long time ago."

"Once a cop, always a cop."

"Got that right," Edgar says. "You betcha."

"Like I said, we're in a hurry," I say. "If I'm right, I've only got a small window of time to try to find Marnee."

Focus, Ed. Please, God, help him focus.

Edgar shifts uneasily in his wheelchair, working his jaw in a tight circle. He has never been a fan of being bullied, to say the least, but even in his diminished state, he must sense my anxiety. "Okay," he says finally. "What do you need to know?"

"Jackie Brentlou, Jacob Gramm. The man Rebecca shot and killed. You remember the case?"

A spark seems to light in his eyes. "How could I forget? Four-flusher got what he had coming to him, you ask me."

"You remember there was one detail about the crime scene we were never able to nail down though. You remember that?"

He stares at me, blinking.

"C'mon, Edgar."

"I don't. Wait a minute. The prints. There were all those muddy boot prints next to the bloodstain we found on the porch of the room at that motel. What was it called, the Virginia Dixie Motor Inn?"

"Right." It comes back to me now as well. I glance at Colin, who is staring at Edgar with rapt attention.

"You remember how we tracked down where the murder took place from that little label on one of the sheets he used to tie her up?" Edgar pats a palm with his fist. "That was good police work, wasn't it?"

"Yes it was."

"So what's the big deal? What do you want to know about those boot prints now for?"

"Did we ever find out who made them? I must have

misplaced a paper or two. I couldn't find anything about it in the file."

Edgar stares some more. Then he surprises me. "Don't you remember, Jer? She was the gal who delivered the newspaper."

It all rushes back. A fidgety, talkative woman. Not bad looking, a little odd maybe. She was living in a house trailer in a park a quarter of a mile off of Hull Street, pair of yappy dogs in the kitchen.

The motor court manager told us he'd seen her wearing gardening boots like that once or twice when she got out of her car. We tracked her down through the circulation department. But nothing ever came from our talking with her. She wasn't even working the week Jackie Brentlou was killed because she was recovering from gallbladder surgery. The newspaper confirmed this. Her gardening boots were a common brand. They matched the prints, but they were fairly new and like the prints bore no distinctive marking. Could have been anybody. End of story, dead end. All in all the prints we're looking at now may not even qualify as the thinnest of threads.

I just can't seem to let the issue go.

"What was that cleaning woman's name, you remember?"

Edgar surprises me again.

"Mary Harper. But what difference does it make? Gramm was the killer."

The television channel has switched from the news to a syndicated rerun of Star Trek, the opening credits with the starship Enterprise bursting through space, like a flicker of lightning.

The moment passes and Edgar's attention is drawn back to the screen. Whatever answers he may have provided, they're not coming back—at least, for now.

I pat him on the shoulder. "I don't know what

difference it will make, E. But I'm glad you remembered the name. Thank you."

"Least I could do." He continues to stare at the screen along with the other men. "Ain't we all seen enough grief for one life?"

Eleven

That was the beginning. After our wee hours discussion that night, Rebecca began working with me on the case of the murdered shipping clerk. Which led to another and another and basically every case from then on.

She set up a little table next to mine in my basement office. On the table were two things: Rebecca's Bible and an old cassette tape recorder. We debriefed each case together. She asked questions and I told her everything I knew so far. She would record everything I told her, so she could sit and play it back again the next day before erasing the tape. Then she would study her Bible and pray, sometimes for an hour or two, even more.

I had a hard time understanding what she was doing at first.

"Why are we spending so much time on this?" I asked one night. "The last thing I want to do when I come home at night is talk any more about the cases I'm working." I was exhausted, physically and emotionally drained.

Rebecca looked hurt. "Okay," she said. "I can just leave you to deal with this yourself."

"No. I didn't mean it like that. I'm sorry. I'm glad you're trying to help."

She looked at me for a long, hard moment. Then she kissed me on the forehead. "Don't worry," she said. "Go ahead and get some sleep."

Soon Rebecca was helping me with nearly all of my cases. She wasn't perfect, of course. Sometimes she made mistakes and I worried her involvement with my work was just her way of seeking revenge for what happened to her and Carlita. Sometimes, too, I wondered if she was only acting as a sounding board for me, if there really was any more to it than her loving and supporting me.

I never breathed a word to my superiors or any other detectives, of course, and certainly not to any prosecutors for fear of tainting any of my cases. Rebecca never visited a crime scene. She never canvassed a neighborhood knocking on doors searching for information and potential witnesses. She never camped out at the morgue waiting for an autopsy result or worked the telephone deep into the night to follow up on a potential lead. She never bothered to learn much about evidence collection, ballistics, or fingerprints, or DNA, either.

She could have sought more attention for herself, but she never did.

Since I've been teaching classes at VCU, I've thought a lot about how Rebecca helped me during those years.

Criminologists often debate about criminogenesis, or the causes of crime. Many academics still adhere to the Chicago School, which argues human behavior is generally more the result of societal factors, physical and economic environments, rather than personal or genetic attributes. Or they may believe the development of delinquent or criminal subcultures, such as gangs, offer a better explanation for criminal activity.

As you might expect, there isn't a lot of discussions within the halls of academia about sin, demons, and believers of whatever stripe praying against them.

Back when I had a full caseload, I would wake up in the middle of the night every now and then to find Rebecca kneeling on the floor with her eyes closed, leaning over the bed beside me.

The first time it happened I was so startled I started to

reach for my gun. Rebecca's opened her eyes and looked at me before closing them again. At first, I thought she was asleep, but then I realized she wasn't sleeping.

She was engaged in combat, a kind I knew too little about.

• • •

"Where to?" Colin backs the car from its parking slot in front of the nursing home.

"Back to the camp." I have just hung up the phone after speaking with Lori. There are no new developments— still no luck locating Alex, though the police are trying. Searchers are still combing the camp hoping to find some additional trace of Marnee. I want to speak with Ford about those boot prints.

At dusk the franchise restaurant lights along Broad Street wink to passersby like sirens of the night. Beyond the passenger window of Colin's Saab, the heat of the day has finally begun to dissipate.

"How many Mary Harpers you think live in Virginia?"

"I don't know," Colin says. "Can't be that many."

"Of course the woman could've easily moved, then we'd be looking at the whole country."

"Or the whole world. If she's still alive."

"Right."

"You really think this has something to do with Marnee, Granddad?"

"It's a lead. We're going to follow it through."

"Marnee talks about you all the time, you know."

Lori has told me the same. The thought makes me smile until I'm reminded of where Marnee might be and what might be happening to her. I'm also reminded of Lori's request before this all happened.

"Your mom tells me you want to move out and go live with your Dad."

"Yup." It's clear from the tone in his voice he's not too happy with the change in subject.

"You think it'd be fun then, living there in the condo with him?"

"I guess. Mom and me just don't see eye to eye most of the time."

"And you think it will be different with your Dad."

"I don't know. He's my father. Where else would I go?"

"I want you to do something for me, Colin."

"Okay."

"When we find Marnee—and we will—there's going to be a lot of fallout, whether your dad has her or not."

"She's not with Dad."

"I know you don't think so, but listen. One way or the other, I want you to promise me you won't do anything right away when it comes to moving out. Wait a while. Give it a couple of months. Can you do that for me?"

He stares at the street ahead for a few moments. "I guess," he says after a while.

We cross Staples Mill Road. The driver of an eighteen-wheeler looks lost, frozen at the light. Colin twists the wheel so as to avoid the big truck.

"You handle the car like a pro."

He snickers.

"You drive a lot?"

"Since Mom and Dad split up, all the time."

Lori must be coming to rely on Colin much of the time. Like picking up Marnee from camp. No wonder she's in a panic about him leaving.

"You think Dad screwed up leaving Mom?" he asks.

"I think he's walking away from the best thing that ever happened in his life. And whether you realize it or not, he's throwing a little bit of you away with your mother too."

Colin says nothing more. We drive on through the gathering darkness, hoping Marnee isn't suffering an even worse fate.

Twelve

*M*y father's name was Daniel Obadiah Strickland. He came to the states with my mother from the British highlands during World War II, was a chain smoker and a drunk and a failure both as a farmer and as a parent. He was a lean, wiry specimen of rock hard muscle and gray eyes that narrowed at the slightest provocation.

"Come on, Jerry. Time for your punishment."

I can still see him standing in the barn stall above my six-year-old back, stick in hand. Work was all we knew on the farm, a modest spread where we also grew corn. Nineteen head of prize Holstein shaped our waking and sleeping, sometimes it seemed, even our very existence.

My father was very successful at maintaining outward order. He saw demons in every legalistic failing or anything else that failed to live up to his own way of looking at the world. His idea of faith was proving he didn't really need God, except as an external means of justifying his own torture of himself and others.

Grace for him simply meant a thicker, stiffer switch cut from one of the saplings behind our barn. Paradoxically, the thicker branches tended to cushion us from more of the force of his blows.

In my younger days I used to ride a Harley Davidson Superglide. When we were first married, Rebecca loved nothing better, besides singing, than riding that bike with me. She begged *me to go as often as we could, and she would whoop and giggle like a schoolgirl at the roar of the engine, the feel of the wind in her hair.*

One afternoon we drove up to the mountains to cruise the Blue Ridge Parkway, a trip we'd often made before. We stopped at an overlook where you could see hawks circling in the distance and the farms in the valley far below formed a perfect mosaic. I did my best that afternoon to describe for her some of the things my father had done to me.

She listened attentively, tears forming in her eyes. She hugged me and kissed me and when I finally finished we held each other. After a while she pointed me toward the valley below. "Jerry," she said softly. "God made all this."

"I know," I said, because I felt it, at least in that moment, more than I ever had before.

"And when we die, there's a far greater beauty waiting for us than any of this."

It was an incredible thing to imagine.

But in my deepest heart and soul where it mattered, I had pretty much stopped thinking about such things. It didn't matter how many times Rebecca or others dragged me to church.

My father suffered from emphysema. One cold winter afternoon not long after he passed away, the old barn he built by hand years before burned clear to the ground. The firemen said faulty wiring caused the fire and it was a miracle the place hadn't gone up in flames before then.

I remember thinking that decrepit wreck of a structure where he had abused himself and us for so many years had just been hanging on, waiting for my old man to go.

• • •

Back at the camp the scene is pretty much what I expect. Floodlights blooming on stanchions. A trailer housing a mobile command post looking out of place in the pale light. Dog teams are working the ground with the scent from the sock, followed by flashlights and searchers.

A state police helicopter with a search light hovers overhead.

We approach the open door of the trailer. Lori sits at a small table inside with her head in her hands and her auburn hair spilling over her temples.

"Hey, sweetie."

She looks up and sweeps her back as we step inside.

"Hey Dad. I'm glad you're back."

We give each other a hug, holding it a little longer than usual. Her voice sounds thin and reedy, as though someone has driven a nail through her psyche. Lori usually holds it together in a traumatic situation. A couple of years before when Colin fractured his tibia playing soccer and required major surgery she coordinated his transport to the hospital from her car on the way from the library to the emergency room while Alex was tied up in court; met everyone at the hospital, discussed the treatment options with the doctors, and stood vigil with Marnee while Colin was in surgery.

But tonight she's been pushed to a different universe.

"Still no word from Alex?"

"Nothing," she says.

"How are you holding up?"

"I'm still here." She dabs with her finger at the corners of her eyes.

"Is Major Ford around?"

"Yes."

"You need to find someplace you can lie down for a couple of minutes. Everyone's doing all they can. Colin and I have been working on something I need to talk with Ford about."

"Maybe. Okay. She hesitates for a moment...Dad?"

"Yeah?"

"These are good people looking for Marnee, right? I mean, they have the best chance of finding her."

"Ford runs a tight ship. And the State Police are already

involved. Colin and I saw the Amber Alert message on television."

"That's good, but maybe we should be calling the FBI or someone else."

You can't really blame her. She wants to fix what is, for the time being at least, unfixable.

"We just have to be patient. It could be a while before we know anything."

She raises her head to search my eyes with hers. "Will it? Don't tell me that, Dad, if you don't really think it's going to be."

"I won't. Trust me, I won't."

She nods.

"Now where's Ford?"

"I think he's out back talking to some of the searchers."

I give Lori a hug and kiss her on the forehead as we take our leave.

I find Ford out back as advertised. He's looking over a clipboard with one of his officers, sweat staining the underarms of his uniform and trickling from his forehead. He finishes with the officer and his eyes take a bead on mine.

"Ground search still negative?"

"Yes," he says. "But we'll keep going through the night. Need to cover every inch of this place."

"Anything else?"

"Got a line on where your son-in-law might have gone. One of his girlfriend's co- workers told us she thought they were heading down to Virginia Beach for the weekend."

"But I thought he was going to be out of cell phone range."

"Could have been a ruse to keep people from trying to contact him."

"You run checks on all the Virginia Beach hotels and house rental agencies?"

"Done. But we came up empty. I've got my best folks out here on this, Jerry."

"Thanks. I appreciate everything you all are doing."

"Anything else you need?" He starts to pull away.

"A couple of things, yeah, if you don't mind. I'm worried about Lori."

"We'll see she gets home or put together some sort of accommodation for her."

"Good. Thank you."

"What else?"

"One more thing. Maybe it's crazy, but I saw something that bothered me out there at the scene where we found Marnee's sock."

"What's that?"

"There was a boot print."

"Yeah, we saw it. Took photos and made a casting."

"Any theories?"

He shrugs. "You probably noticed there is new construction going on next door. We figure it must have come from one of the workers. We're trying to get in touch with the contractor, see if we can come up with a list of all the subs and crew who may have been on site. That's about as far as we've gotten."

"The print seemed pretty small for a man though, don't you think?"

"Could have been a man with small feet or maybe even a woman. Why?"

"The boot print reminded of one from a case a long time ago."

"Well, it's a little unusual, but not that uncommon a boot, I think."

"I know."

"What case are you talking about?"

"The Jackie Brentlou murder."

Ford raises an eyebrow and stares at me for a moment.

"Brentlou. You mean the one who—?"

"Yeah, that's the one."

Listening to myself, I'm sure it sounds crazy. Even Colin looks uncomfortable.

"I'll keep it in mind, Jerry. I know you're trying to help. We're all under a lot of stress right now. Why don't you head on home and try and to get some sleep? We'll call you right away if anything happens."

"Just humor me on this, Hal. Will you please?"

Someone motions to him from across the parking lot, and he looks that way for a second. "Sure. Like I said, I'll keep it in mind."

I stare after him as he turns and walks away up the hill.

✤

Thirteen

Here is the problem with trying to remember someone long dead. Eventually, you start forgetting the little details. You start feeling more and more disconnected, as if your memory of the person worked like one long conveyer belt of time instead of the beautifully organic and spontaneous random access machine it was meant to be.

Rebecca always loved to surprise me.

One beautiful Saturday morning when we first married, I came downstairs from sleeping late after a particularly long night working a case in Church Hill to find a picnic lunch and a bottle on the kitchen counter all packed up and ready to go.

"Byrd Park," she said. She was standing at the sink with her back to me, rinsing pots and pans.

"Yeah?"

"Let's take the bike. You and your pretty, devoted wife. No phone, no pager. A little peace, quiet, and solitude. And maybe a boat ride on the lake."

"Sounds perfect." By this point, I had maneuvered up to the sink and wrapped my arms around her from behind.

She smiled. "Don't get any ideas, big boy. It's a semi-public place."

"I thought you said solitude," I said.

"Not that kind of solitude. Maybe later."

I grinned, kissing her neck. "Okay then." I drew back

and reached for a coffee mug from the cabinet overhead.

She finished rinsing the last of the pots, picked up a dishtowel and began drying. "You sleep okay?"

I shrugged. "The usual."

"You were tossing and turning, you know. Especially a couple of hours after you came in and fell asleep. You have a nightmare?"

"Not that I remember."

"Well, it sure seemed like some kind of bad dream to me."

"Trust me, all of last night was a bad dream."

"That ugly, huh?"

I nodded. I reached across to the coffee pot and poured myself a cup. "Can I help you with those dishes?"

"No, you sit and enjoy your coffee. I'm almost through here anyway."

I sat at the kitchen table and took a sip from the mug. Rebecca finished wiping the last of the pans and put it away in the cupboard. She dried off her hands and joined me at the table, kissing me on the cheek as she settled into her chair.

"You're not drinking coffee?"

"Already had my quota for the morning. I drink anymore, I'm liable to take the dishes back out of the cupboard and start washing them all over again."

I chuckled. "Wouldn't want to miss the picnic."

"Not on your life."

"What time is it?" I had left my watch in the bedroom and in my haste to get to the coffee had neglected to look at the clock in the hall.

"After eleven, I think."

"Man." I shook my head. "Guess I really needed the sleep."

Rebecca put her hand on my arm. "You deserve it," she said.

I said nothing. Outside, a patch of beautiful spring sky was visible through the screen. I found myself looking out the window, unable to keep from focusing on it.

"Is this really who you are, Jerry Strickland?"

"What?"

"All the time you put in. All the chasing after bodies, victims, and murderers. You know what I mean. Is this really what you want out of life?"

I was taken aback. I looked at her over the top of my cup as I drank. "It's what I do," I said, probably sounding more defensive than I intended.

She didn't seem too happy with my answer. "I know it's what you do, but is it really what you want?" She pulled her hand from my arm and stared at me for a long moment.

"I don't know if it's what I want. I mean, not ultimately. No one's ever asked me that before."

"You're still young."

"I feel older than I am."

"That's what I mean, but there's still time. You should go back to school."

"Maybe. But I love being a cop."

"Really?"

"Really."

"You get scared sometimes?"

"Yes."

"Not just about how you might be injured or killed but about what might be happening to your soul, how much darkness it can stand?"

"Enough, I guess, to try to set some things right."

"Setting some things right—is that what it's all about?"

"I suppose."

"And this is what makes you happy?"

"Most of the time. Maybe being a detective is about the closest I can get."

"Closest to what?"

"I don't know, truth?"

She smiled, although I remember thinking it seemed a sad smile. Maybe my response had been too flippant.

But she said: "Once a cop, always a cop. Isn't that what they say?"

I took another sip of my coffee. "Something like that."

Our eyes met for another moment. "All right, then," she said. "I just wanted to be sure."

Cops are different than most people. You don't think the same about your mortality when you're only one bad situation away from the reaper. I once heard a police chaplain say every cop knows they might be pinning on their final hallelujah with their badge, whether they try to push it away or not.

Lots of others guys on the force came from a long line of policemen. Their fathers were cops, sometimes even their grandfathers.

Not mine.

Just before he died, my father called me into his bedroom at the farm, his eyes bulbous and bloodshot, his skin doughy and sallow.

"This place won't ever make a go of it, Jerry. I want you and Paul to get out of here. Go on someplace else, do something different, and make your own way."

In his own awkward manner, I guess, the old man was trying to apologize for all the pain he put me through.

My father barely scratched a living off his pitiful piece of land. In a way, maybe that's all I was ever reaching for, too. To scratch some bits of truth from the land of the living on behalf of the broken and the dead. Like just about every other cop I'd ever known. Before the blue hallelujah came to put an end to whatever bright line between right and wrong we were trying to plant ourselves on.

• • •

"That big cop thinks you've got Alzheimer's or something," Colin says after Ford leaves.

"Thanks for the, what is it you kids call it? The 411?"

"You got it."

"What if he's right?"

"I don't think you've got Alzheimer's."

"Good thing. You tell me if that changes. Deal?"

"Deal."

We hang around the camp a little longer, but it soon becomes apparent, at least for the time being, there is nothing more for us to do but wait. Despite all advice to the contrary, Lori has decided to keep a vigil in the command post.

"Why don't you head on back to your place with Colin again?" she tells me. "There's a cot over here in the corner and I may lay down for a few minutes. I'll call you if something happens."

I understand her feelings. The camp's the last place anyone saw Marnee, and Lori needs to somehow keep a grip on that.

"Is there anything we can get for you?"

She takes hold of my hand. "No, Dad. You've done more than enough for now. I appreciate you coming all the way out here again and trying to help and all..."

We say our good-byes, Colin and I climb back in the Saab.

On the way back to the house, I trying to think where else we might go from here, but other than the shaky boot print idea, I come up blank. Maybe Ford is right. Maybe I should just forget about trying to intervene and pray Ford, his team, and the State Police can find Marnee in time.

If it were back in the old days, I'd start running a background and cross check on all the Mary Harpers I could find, starting in Richmond, then in Virginia and beyond, until I found the right one. But the old days are long gone. I'm sure I can get Colin to start searching online, but to what end? We don't want to waste anyone's time. Ford and his people have enough on their hands right now.

We don't talk much during the drive. I doze off a couple of times. A few blocks from my house, the familiar entrance to my neighborhood takes on a deceptively innocent cast this time of night.

As we pull into my empty driveway. Two houses down, there appears to be some kind of party in progress. Cars fill the driveway, spill over onto the lawn, and several more line each side of the street.

"Life goes on," I say to no one in particular.

"They must watch the news. You think they know about Marnee and that she's related to you?"

"I'm sure they don't have a clue. The only people I still talk to on this street are the Menheimers next door."

The neighborhood has started to go downhill these past couple of years. A less respectable crowd has moved in. We even had a shooting last month in front of the corner market where I've been buying my meat for years.

"Maybe I should go say something to them."

"Don't waste your breath."

"Okay."

I pull out my house key and push open the car door.

What the heck, I decide. Once inside the house, I might as well dust off the computer and get Colin to start it up for me, maybe put him to work on the Mary Harper thing while I catch some shuteye. At least it's something.

"Granddad?"

"Yes."

"Can I talk to you about something?"

"Of course."

"There's something I haven't told anybody. I don't think it really means anything but—"

"What's that?"

"This morning, when I drove Marnee to her camp, she dropped a piece of paper from her shorts pocket as she was getting out of the car. I found it when I pulled into the lot for my job at the pool. It got wedged between her seat and the door."

"What was it?"

He reaches into his pocket and pulls out a crinkled section of a piece of paper. "I think it's part of a note."

"A note?"

He hands me the piece of paper, or what's left of it. The fragment has been torn from a larger sheet. Written in black ink are the words 'Don't tell your mother. She's got enough to worry about.'

I stare at the handwriting and read it again. "You know for sure Marnee was carrying this on her person?"

"Yeah. I found it when I was opening the passenger door to pull my backpack out of the back. It wasn't there when I put the backpack on the seat. It must've come from her."

"Who do you think it's from?"

"Don't you recognize the writing?"

I shake my head.

"It's from my dad."

Oh, boy.

"Why didn't you tell anyone about this sooner?"

"I didn't want to get Dad in trouble."

"We need to show this to the police and to your mother."

"Wait. I'm not sure you're going to be up for this, but do you want to take another ride? A little longer one, this time."

"A longer one? At this time of night? What are you talking about?"

"We need to go to Virginia Beach."

"Virginia Beach?"

"Yeah."

"Why?"

"I think I know where my dad might be."

Fourteen

The girl rouses in the middle of the night, but not too much as the old man plunges the syringe into her arm.

He has moved her down to the basement where he has positioned a cot in an empty back room. The chamber has no windows and solid concrete walls, and is virtually soundproof. One of his tenants used to keep his big dog in here during the day when neighbors complained the barking had became too loud. But just to be certain, the old man has turned down all the thermostats in the house above to keep the central air conditioning constantly running and has positioned a loud dehumidifier unit in the room.

He removed the gag earlier, gave the girl a cup of water to drink, and sat her on the toilet so she could empty her bladder before carrying her down the stairs. She stared at him the entire time with empty eyes. He's sure she'll remember nothing.

He stood her on a bathroom scale for a moment as well and calculates her weight at about seventy pounds. This fresh round of drugs should buy him several more hours to execute the next phase of his plan.

The girl's hands and feet are chained to the cot. He checks the handcuffs again to make certain they are secure. Then he rolls her head to the side for a moment and opens her mouth to make sure she is breathing regularly and her airway is clear.

It's a shame really, he thinks. A shame he had to take her the way he did, a shame for what he must do next.

Kids these days have no discipline, no respect. No one guiding them with a firm hand, correcting their mistakes, or watching over them when they need it most.

Curiosity may have killed the cat. He hopes it won't come down to that with the girl. But he's come this far already.

He stops for a moment and looks at his hands. He almost doesn't recognize them; hasn't, in fact, since this whole thing started. What has gotten hold of him? A dark burden is filling his life. He realizes with a shiver it has always been there.

He flexes his shoulders to chase the thought away.

Facing the girl, he lays his medical bag on the bed, and then positions a thick towel, waterproof sheet, and a wad of bandages beneath her foot. He turns the bare toes toward him.

He's not completely sure about the anesthetic effects of the drugs he's given her. It's just one more risk of the many he's had to take.

Pausing, he takes a deep breath. Whatever he has to do. He reaches into his bag for the surgical tool.

• • •

Two hours later, we are in a State Police cruiser heading for Virginia Beach.

We didn't have to tell Ford much in order to set everything into motion. Colin has described a beach house where he thinks Alex might be staying. It's back from the dunes a ways on an isolated stretch of sand somewhere between Sandbridge and the northern Outer Banks, accessible only by Dune Buggy or four wheel drive at low tide. He says he doesn't remember there being any telephone or television or anything. Sounds about as private as you can get.

"Dad's got a client who lets him use the house sometimes," Colin told him.

Figures. But I also wonder if it's the type of place Alex would take Marnee if he has her.

Lori wanted to accompany us, but Ford said no. I would have liked to have her with us, but I see Ford's logic in wanting to avoid a potential confrontation between estranged husband and wife. After a lengthy discussion, Lori agreed to be transported by a separate car a half an hour or so behind.

Leaning against the rear door window with my head tucked inside my jacket, I sleep for a good portion of the ride. One minute we are passing down the peninsula toward Williamsburg, and the next, it seems, we are already sailing along the Virginia Beach expressway between Norfolk and the high-rise-lined oceanfront. Staring out through the glass, I feel years younger. Maybe it's the call of the sea.

Colin, for his part, peers out through the glass on his side no doubt feeling a mixture of heightened stature and apprehension over potentially confronting his father.

It's late and getting later by the time we pull into the parking lot behind a state police division headquarters on Military Highway in Chesapeake. The plan calls for us to convoy with a couple of locally based troopers to the beach at the Southern tip of Sandbridge where we will hook up with a squad of local Sheriff's deputies and VA Beach Police in 4 wheel drive vehicles. Since it's nearly pitch dark, the search will be slow-going. Colin says he remembers the house being about five or six miles from the end of the paved road.

"Mr. Strickland, our instructions are to accompany you and this young man here, with the young man's guidance, to a beach residence where his father may be hiding and may be keeping his sister," says the captain in charge of the operation from the front seat of the cruiser as we head out.

He is a straight-laced type with close cropped hair and dressed, like the other troopers in the car, in dark blue fatigues.

"That's the long and short of it. Of course the operative word here is may."

"Yes, sir."

"How long do you think it will take us from here?"

"Depends how long it takes us to get down the beach in the dark. The surf's pretty strong tonight, which will help cover our approach. We'll go with low running lights so we don't spook anybody. At least the tide is working in our favor. It'll be at it's lowest in another hour."

"Good timing then."

"One thing's for sure. If what your grandson tells us is correct, Mr. Butler's not going to be running out on us. Unless he has a helicopter stashed away somewhere."

At the off-ramp where the pavement turns to sand, we meet up with the deputies and a Virginia Beach SWAT unit, who are waiting for us in a trio of SUVs with their tires already partially deflated for running on the beach.

The black ocean looms before us. Large white warning signs with bold red letters warn drivers of the potential hazards of beach driving. The crash of white-capped breakers reaches our ears.

Overhead, a sliver of a moon skids between fast moving clouds, but it fails to provide much light. It's still humid, but the air is much cooler. A gusty salt breeze shivers the dry grasses along the dunes. After a quick transfer into one of the waiting SUVs, we move in tandem down the beach.

It's a bone-jarring ride. The sand is wide enough for us to pass with the tide out, but there are only a couple of narrow tire tracks to follow, easily veered away from in the dark, and the resulting jolts to the tires and shocks bounce the SUVs around like a minor earthquake. My hips begin to feel like one giant toothache.

Colin pipes up after a few minutes. "The more I think about it, the more I know Dad's got to be here. I remember him telling me when he comes down here he just sort of forgets about the world."

Maybe he should be doing some more of that kind of forgetting with your mother, I want to tell him, but don't.

"You want to climb up front here and help keep a watch out with us, Colin?" the captain says after a while longer. "We should be getting closer to the target."

Colin pulls himself from the back seat beside me and clambers up into the passenger seat across from the captain. The other team members in the vehicle shift to make room and fill the empty space, their gear rattling and clinking as the vehicle lurches forward.

"I'm told you worked homicide years ago," the captain says, as if he needs to show he's not ignoring me. The man has forearms the size of half-gallon jugs, one of which drapes calmly across the back of the seat.

"Been a decade or two. I teach criminal science now."

He nods without looking back. "Way I hear it you were one of the best."

"I had a lot of help."

"Sure." The SWAT captain smiles, baring his teeth in the dim light reflected from the dash.

We continue down the beach another half a mile or so until Colin begins to look off to his right, straining to see across the darkened dunes.

"I think this is it," he says. "I remember that stand of trees and the way the beach curves in a little right here. We're real close."

The captain squawks his radio twice. The caravan slows to a crawl. I sit up in my seat. From inside the vehicle with the windows rolled up we've been insulated from the smells and sounds of the beach, but now the driver powers all the windows down.

We splash slowly through some salt backwash and pull to a stop. The driver kills the engine and cuts off the parking lights. The roar of a motor drifts through the darkness toward us from somewhere up ahead.

The captain reaches up and flips a switch on the dome light to prevent it from turning on as he pushes open his door. "Anybody got any idea what that sound is?"

"Yeah." Colin is right behind him through the door, scrambling out and onto the sand. "It's this big generator thing. Dad ran it most of the time when I was here to power the air conditioning and the water and the lights."

"So somebody's home then."

I shove my door open and, using the ceiling strap and my free hand as a lever, hoist myself up and out of the car along with everyone else. The night and the ocean whirl around me for a moment.

"Does the public ever use this stretch of beach?"

"Hardly ever," the captain says. "There's a gate at the northernmost end of the outer banks and the state border. Residents there can use it to get out in case of emergency or evacuation, but otherwise, this area is all supposed to be protected and undeveloped."

"Unless you know people in high places."

The captain nods. "This place was probably built years ago."

The other two vehicles have pulled to a stop behind us. They cut their engines, too, and couple of sheriff's deputies and a VA Beach SWAT team clamber onto the beach, ten men and one woman. With their military style gear, they would be impressive in any setting, but here they seem especially so. I hope their skills won't be needed.

The captain gathers the assembled team and gives them instructions in a low even voice. I hear mention of air support. Apparently, an observation chopper has taken up station a few miles downrange, waiting to find out if they will be needed. All in all, this seems like a well-organized take down, if that's what it becomes.

Colin and I are told to stay with the vehicles; one of the deputies is assigned to wait with us while the remaining members of the team fan out down the beach, moving quickly to surround the property.

"Won't be long now," I tell Colin.

"I hope Dad isn't mad at me."

"Mad or not, he won't have time to think about it once he finds out why we're here, especially if he's got your sister."

The deputy assigned to wait with us stands silently by the SUV's front bumper. A gust of wind swirls down the beach and stirs the dune grass. The undertow and waves keep up their ceaseless roar.

A couple of minutes later, the captain's head appears over top of one of the dunes. He waves his hand, giving the all clear.

"What's happening?" Colin asks.

"I don't know," the deputy says. "But I guess it's okay for us to head on in."

We follow him down the beach until the house becomes visible. It sits back from the ocean a ways, and there is a pathway through the dunes leading toward a back deck. The lights are all ablaze inside.

Alex is clearly visible as we approach, standing on the deck talking with the captain and the group of assembled officers, dressed in his bathrobe. A young woman with long blonde hair flanks him. She is clad in a robe as well, her bare legs crossed and seated at a table in an embarrassed pose.

The captain raises his walkie-talkie to his mouth and says something into it. The SWAT team appears to have stood down.

Closing in on the house, I can make out Alex's face, his high forehead and athletic, chiseled chin and cheeks.

The look in his eyes is grave. We reach the base of the deck and begin to mount the stairs.

"Colin, Jerry," Alex calls out. "What in the world's going on? What's this they're telling me about Marnee being missing?"

Fifteen

*H*elping me took a toll on Rebecca. The long nights of talking and worrying over homicide case details I sometimes think she never should have known. Somehow we always managed to come out whole.

Until the killing of Jackie Brentlou.

A hundred yards into midnight, the Brentlou girl's half-hidden body surfaced in the beams of our flashlights, a ghostly image of an arm and a hand blooming from beneath the water in a macabre collage.

The current was swift and powerful this time of year on the James. Edgar and I needed to watch our footing. Henrico County Marine Patrol had two boats on station. They'd secured the body with a dredging net, but I'd asked if Edgar and I could take a look before they pulled her out.

"Somebody went to a lot of trouble weighing her down with that log," Edgar said.

"Brilliant, E." I kicked at the splintered top of wood that had surfaced against a boulder. It failed to budge.

"I'm just saying, that's all. You sure we need to be doing this, Jerry? Those rapids look pretty gnarly. Last thing I need is a cold swim in the dark."

He scratched at a patch of sunburn on his arm, impatience leaking into his morose twang. His skin, in contrast to the pale corpse, glowed crimson from a long spring weekend at the beach, his bulbous eyelids owl-like, his cheeks hollowed with fatigue.

"Just trying to get a feel for—"What? I couldn't say exactly. These were the moments when I could feel Rebecca acting with and through me, the times when I chose to examine whatever circumstances presented themselves through something other than just my intellect. In truth, there was no earthly reason why Edgar and I needed to risk life and limb perched among the rocks in the middle of the swiftly-flowing James after dark in order to take a peek at a victim who had long since achieved ambient temperature. Some might accuse me of grandstanding.

In the normal drill I should have been playing the scientist. I should have already begun examining the case through a microscope. But I'd made sure we'd disembarked at the back of a funhouse mirror instead, accentuated by the confusing mist swirling through the glow from the River Patrol flood lamps. All we lacked for this corpse scene was the unsettling accompaniment of the typical air force of flies.

"What are you thinking?" Edgar asked.

I said nothing.

Earlier, when I got the call out, Rebecca had somehow known exactly whom we'd be pulling out of the river.

That's what had me clinging to this boulder in the middle of the pitch darkness of the river, one foot propped against the gunwale of our anchored boat, no matter there wasn't much to see. That's what had my frayed nerves strung tight as piano wire.

A line of police cruisers idled along the bank of the river, blue beacons swirling, the tick of their warm engines swallowed by the sounds of the James.

"Are we through? Can we please go ahead and let these people do their jobs now?" Edgar glanced back over his shoulder at river patrol, whispering and smoking cigarettes in their boat.

I pointed at the water. "You see how carefully those knots are tied to the concrete block pulling down her hands?"

"Yeah."

"Our perp's a tactician. Careful. Or sadistic. Look at the side of her head."

Edgar squinted at a black knot of tissue below her hairline. "God," he said. "She's missing an ear."

"This wasn't some amateur who made a mistake then panicked and threw her body into the water. If the current wasn't so strong here and she didn't happened to catch on this log just the way she did, her body'd be almost to the mouth of the Chesapeake by now and an entrée' for sharks."

"So we caught a break then."

"I want to go over the lists of everyone she's ever known, any one who might have had any contact with her."

He nodded. "Hey, Jer, you know it could just as well have been some random dirtbag."

"We'll see," I said. "We'll see."

• • •

I sit between Lori and Colin in the perp seat of yet another state police cruiser on the way back to Richmond. The Plexiglas barrier is pulled shut. Our driver, a young trooper with a glistening shaved head and Bluetooth receiver attached to one ear, seems more interested in talking to someone on the phone than in our mess.

The sojourn to Virginia Beach has turned out to be a waste of time. Alex seems genuinely clueless about Marnee's disappearance. He asked a lot of questions, naturally, but kept wanting to bring the discussion back around to what was being done to find Marnee. He sounded more like a worried parent than a kidnapper, which is the worst of all news. A stranger has most likely taken Marnee.

Lori notices me looking at her.

"What now, Dad?"

I shake my head. "I don't know."

I try to think objectively about everything we have seen so far, but my thoughts are a tangled mess. I keep coming back to the boot prints and Edgar and the past, and I see nothing else but a black hole. I don't want to burden Lori with random, maybe false hopes of answers where they may be none yet.

Lori went through so much when Rebecca went to
prison: the shock of losing her mother, not to mention the
taunts a teenage daughter of a felon had to endure in school.
Is she going to have to live though a different nightmare
now? How much can one person be expected to take?

"Are you okay?" I ask.

She shakes her head. "You saw who he was with." Her
face is drawn, haggard- looking.

"You mean Alex."

She nods.

"I saw."

"I was pretty sure he's moved on, been sleeping with
this other woman. I knew it, but—" Her fist pounds softly
against the car door.

"It still stings." I reach up and wipe a tear away from
her face.

"Maybe he wasn't sleeping with her," Colin says. Maybe
there's some other reason why they were together."

Lori glares at him. "How can you still sit there and
defend him after what you just saw? Didn't you see her
showing off her legs from beneath that robe? What are you,
blind?"

"I'm sorry, Mom. I . . . " His words seem to fade into
oblivion.

"I just want her back," Lori tries to hold back a sob. "I
just want Marnee back."

My arms are wedged at my side. As gently as I can, I
lift them over my head and extend them to put one arm
around her shoulders, pulling her close, and the other over
Colin's broad back.

"I'm sorry," Lori says to no one in particular. "Sorry
about the whole thing, sorry about this whole mess."

We ride that way for a while in silence, and I close my
eyes against the dark.

• • •

I sleep then, a deeper sleep than I ever remember. It is as if the world has been replaced by some alternate reality. I catch fleeting glimpses of Rebecca and Lori, Colin and Marnee, and I am somewhere flying at night. Marnee's voice calls out to me. Not the Marnee of today but the-little-girl-on-the-sidewalk Marnee. What is it about her that flows through all of us? What mysteries have knitted us together as a family?

All at once I am on a darkened Richmond street, and I am young again, back in the days when I still worked patrol. Marnee, or a young girl that looks very much like her, stands in the dusky gloom of an alleyway as my partner and I are patrolling past. I recognize the area, but it's not in the city. Off Midlothian Turnpike maybe. Somewhere Southside. My partner stops the car and I leap from the car, giving chase after the girl's fleeting shadow, but I never catch up.

• • •

The room is light when I awaken. I am at home under the covers in my own bed, still in the same clothes I wore the night before. The windows are closed for a change; someone has turned on the air conditioning. Morning sunlight slants through an opening in the shades.

"Dad?"

Lori stretches herself awake in the chair across the room. For a moment, I think I must have dreamed everything. The drive to the camp and the frantic search for Marnee. The long ride to Virginia Beach and the darkened journey up the sand. But turning my head, I see Colin stretched out on a line of pillows on the floor fast asleep.

"How'd I get here?"

"You were out cold, so we carried you in here and stretched you out on the bed."

"Any word about Marnee?"

"None." She has two phones propped in the chair beside her: my old portable handset and her sleek mobile.

"The nurse was here a couple of hours ago," she says. "She says you need to rest."

I feel rested enough. I raise my head up off the pillow. "I just need something to eat, that's all. And maybe some coffee, if you don't mind. I can help you make it."

Lori almost smiles. "No, no. I can handle it. It'll give me something to take my mind off of things."

"What time is it?"

"After nine o'clock. You've been sleeping since we brought you back here around three."

Below me, Colin breaths heavily in his slumber but twitches restlessly, as if wrestling demons.

"What about you? Did you get any sleep?"

"A little maybe. Not really."

I feel guilty for having conked out on her.

"Where's Alex?"

"Talking with the police at our, I mean, my house, I think. I left them there to come back over here about six. Alex's girlfriend made herself scarce, wouldn't you know. A policewoman drove me back over here."

"Anyone still out at the camp?"

"Yes. There are still people searching for evidence," she says. "They've called in the FBI. I think the focus has shifted now that we know Alex doesn't have her."

"Where's Major Ford?"

"At the house with Alex, I think." Her mouth quivers as she speaks, pulling against the sunken shadows of her eyes.

"You need to try to get some rest, Lori." I reach my hand out and she places hers in mind.

"I know." She wipes a tear from her eye with her free hand and suppresses a sniffle. "But I can't." She takes her hand away from mine and pushes herself up from her chair. "Let me go cook those eggs for you."

"Thank you." I struggle to pull myself upright on the pillow. "Leave the phone, will you?"

"Dad, you're supposed to stay quiet, remember?"

"I know, but I need to talk to Ford. It's important."

She stares at me for a moment or two before bending down and placing my home phone handset on the bed beside me. "Do you even know his number?"

"Not off the top of my head. But I was hoping you could supply it."

She sighs, pressing some buttons on her mobile phone to come up with the number and reading it off to me, before stepping from the room.

I pick up the phone and punch in the number. I'm not some hallucinogenic old cowboy who thinks I am going to be able to come up with some kind of breakthrough on my own. With the FBI taking jurisdiction, I want to talk to Ford before they elbow him out of the way. The Feds may be the experts in this sort of thing, but Hal and I go back a long way. I'd stack his judgment against theirs anytime. I used to be on pretty good terms with the director of the FBI field office over on Parham Road, but last I heard he was transferred out to California.

Ford answers on the third ring. "Mrs. Butler?"

"No, Hal, it's Jerry."

Colin stirs in his sleeping bag on the floor.

"Hey, Jerry. Glad to hear your voice. I was just about to dial your daughter."

"You were? She just stepped into the kitchen for a moment."

Ford says nothing.

"What's happening over there?'

Ford still says nothing. Finally: "You probably heard the Feds are on the case."

"I heard."

"They've got one of their local evidence response units working the camp location and a CARD team arrived here at the house an hour ago from D.C. But listen, that's not why I was about to call your daughter." He seems to hesitate for a moment. "Can you put Mrs. Butler on the phone?"

"I can go get her. But whatever you've got to tell her, Hal, you can tell me."

"Right." He seems to say these words to someone else. "Okay, well look, Jer, maybe it's better if you break the news to her. Things are moving fast here as of a few minutes ago."

"What?" I sit up a little higher in bed. The game has obviously changed. "What do you mean?" I can hear someone yelling in the background. "Did you find Marnee?"

"No," he says. "But the Feds just took a call from someone claiming to be the kidnapper."

Sixteen

Jacob Gramm shared at least one thing with Rebecca: they both had a gift for music. Gramm taught brass in the Henrico County public schools. His specialty was French horn. He rotated through many of the area middle and high schools and was said to be quite an accomplished player.

Jackie Brentlou spent four months learning to play the French horn under Gramm's tutelage at her school, but never took to the instrument, partly, her mother said, because of her refusal to practice. Her parents returned the instrument to the store where'd they'd rented it, which is where it may have lain forgotten had Rebecca not eventually made the connection to point me toward Jacob Gramm.

We were in the living room after dinner listening to a recording of Maria Callas singing O Mio Babbino Caro when a troubled look darkened Rebecca's face.

"Stop," she said.

"What is it?"

"Take me to the school."

"What school?"

"Jackie Brentlou's."

"Why?"

"I have a strong feeling about it."

"Honey, I don't think—"

"No, please. We need to go."

Jackie's school was across town and across the river from

where we lived, but her body had only been discovered a few days before, and a lot of Richmond parents were still on edge.

So I did as she asked and we drove to the school. It was a modern concrete and glass structure typical of the new construction at the time. There were still several cars in the parking lot when we arrived. As it so happened, the football team was doing spring drills on a field beside the school and the marching band was apparently just finishing up a practice as well.

"Where do you want to go?" I asked.

"The band room," she said.

"The band room."

"Yes, please."

I took her inside, and we easily found the music wing by following a few of the band members, not a few of which looked at us with awkward curiosity, though they must have just assumed we were one of the other band member's parents.

The music wing had been built into a hillside, and there were no windows in the band's big practice room, except for a couple of small ones high on the back wall above a large semi-circle of risers.

"What are we doing here, Rebecca?"

"May I just sit down in here for a minute?"

A grand piano, two tympanis, and a bass drum stood to one side. I helped her to the first of the risers, then stood leaning against a bass drum while Rebecca sat in one of the practice chairs.

Rebecca couldn't have known it at the time but Jacob Gramm had been seated in one of those chairs just a couple of days before teaching a trombone class to a group of seventh grade boys. The room had mostly cleared out by then, but a few players were still gathering together their things while Rebecca, apparently oblivious both to me and the students coming and going around her, closed her eyes.

I waited a minute before saying anything. "Honey, you're starting to creep me out a little here."

Rebecca opened her eyes again and said: "I'm sorry, you're right. Let's head on home."

I'd experienced enough of her premonitions and feelings by then not to take them lightly. So after dropping her back home, I went straight back to work. I called Edgar and told him someone from the school system had mentioned Jackie Brentlou might have played a musical instrument or sung in the chorus at one time and I wanted to follow up on it.

It took a couple more days of digging for things to begin to fall in place. Since Jackie had quit playing the horn some time before, her parents had almost forgotten about the experience; they hadn't thought her short-lived musical career would be in any way relevant to her killing. They couldn't even remember Gramm's name or supply the names of any others with whom she may have come in contact in the music department. But a check of school records began to point us in the right direction.

Once we established Jackie played the horn, we ended up interviewing the head of the music department, a handful of faculty members and several student musicians from Jackie's school. The second teacher we talked to was Jacob Gramm.

• • •

South of Quantico the old man squints through the morning sunlight at the long lines of oncoming D.C. commuters driving north on I-95. The Beemer still glides on cruise control at the posted speed limit. He nods from lack of sleep. It's been years since he's had to push himself this hard.

He has barely slept since learning about the girl. His whole life with Carol—investments, pension with benefits, the boat, golf and wintering at their condo in Florida—all threatening to come crashing down because of one stupid mistake with that insaniac Gramm a lifetime ago.

Gramm, the charismatic drinker who regaled him with stories the first time they met at that piece-of-crap watering hole down in Petersburg.

He was just a low level civilian GS 6 working in logistics at Ft. Lee way back then, and Gramm was bigger than life. He was five years into his humdrum first marriage with bills to pay and nothing to do but get older. Gramm was smart, brilliant even. When he ran into him a second time the next night outside the bar, the roll in the hay with the young thing Gramm proposed seemed harmless enough.

He was in over his head. Way over.

The old man believed he'd long since left what happened that night behind him. The excitement of it all until he realized the girl was incapacitated. Gramm's escalating violence and the blood. His own drunken panic, and fear Gramm might try to kill him as well, snatches of a memory of helping to dispose of the body.

He lived in constant fear for weeks afterward. But when he read in the paper Gramm had been shot and killed by the cop's wife, and about all the other things Gramm was suspected of doing, he felt he'd been given a new lease on life.

He knew he should have come forward then and confessed his role in the killing, but he was never able to work up the courage, and as the years rolled by it became easier and easier to ignore. The girl was dead and gone and Gramm was dead and gone. Nothing he could do would ever change that. He even reinvented the scenario in his mind at times. Like a dream he wasn't sure really happened.

He thought he'd made his peace with his Lord and built a decent life for himself enjoying his hard-earned retirement. Until the phone call from the girl's father brought it all rushing back.

He has to keep a clear head. The call was a good first step. The father is a wild card, but manageable, he hopes.

Worst case scenario, there is a little beach town in Mexico he visited with Carol more than ten years ago, and a woman he met at the bar one night when Carol was sick in bed with a migraine. The woman still sends him postcards, written in her broken English. They arrive every other month or so in the post office box he has always kept for correspondence and things he doesn't want Carol to know. He's written back a few times.

That would never be his first choice, of course. It makes him sad to even think about the possibility of leaving Carol and the rest of his life behind. But one thing he knows for sure. He is never going to prison, not at his age.

He shudders for a second, surprised by a Virginia State Police cruiser tucked behind a knoll in the median. He checks his speedometer and glances in his mirror. The cruiser doesn't budge. Idiot cop. Who knows what other manner of mischief is driving right past the guy's nose this morning while he sits collecting a few paltry speeding ticket fines?

He glances at his watch, thinking about the girl back in the basement in Richmond. She should still be asleep, at least for another three or four hours. Up ahead, he spots an exit sign. If he can find a safe place to park, he might just be able to catch an hour of sleep himself before heading south again.

Seventeen

Lori and the kids still occupy the house off of River Road where she and Alex used to live together with Marnee and Colin. As we turn the corner in Colin's Saab, we pass a TV news van at the curb. The driveway is filled with official-looking vehicles. From inside a dark van a tangle of black wires spills across the lawn like a snake slithering toward the house to escape the rising heat.

The home is an upscale brick colonial with large white columns framing the entryway. The front of the house sits at a slight angle to the street to accent the landscaping and the terrain. The edge of a swing set and part of Marnee's old playhouse are visible through a split rail fence around back.

Colin surveys the scene as we move toward the front door. "Mom. Where are we going to come up with so much money?"

The caller has apparently made a ransom demand of five hundred thousand dollars. This is actually the most hopeful news I have heard so far. A kidnapper motivated by money is less likely to harm Marnee.

"Don't bother yourself about the money."

"Why'd he take Marnee? Why'd he come after us? I mean, it's not like we're mega- rich or anything."

"I don't know, sweetheart."

"Use my college money. Use it all; I don't care. I can work my way through school, I can do whatever."

"We'll cross that bridge when we come to it. You let your Father and me worry about those things."

The front door has been left open a crack. We follow the wires sluicing through the entrance into the foyer. The inside of the house has been transformed into a bunker-like headquarters. I've seen its likes before, but never with so many laptops and other computers. Hal Ford is seated with a balding man, a sharply dressed woman, and Alex at the dining room table, which has been covered with dark cloth and turned into an ad hoc briefing table. Alex sports khakis and a blue Polo shirt. Tortoise-shell reading glasses dangle on a chain from his neck and a solid gold power watch big enough to choke a golden retriever fits snuggly around his oversized wrist. Everyone rises as we enter.

Lori ignores Alex and addresses the law enforcement types. "Any more news?"

Ford and the other man shake their heads. From the stranger's suits and mannerisms I take them to be FBI. The woman looks with sympathetic concern at Lori. The balding man gives off an aura of being in control; his features are still angular and athletic well into middle age. The woman looks equally fit but younger in her well tailored suit. Her dark hair is chopped short and, perhaps because of her smaller stature, the Sig Sauer in her waist holster appears to stand out more than do the guns carried by the men.

I make a beeline to baldy.

"You in charge now?"

He looks me up and down. "That's correct. I'm Agent Markinson, FBI Richmond field office. You must be the grandfather."

"That's right."

"Retired cop."

I nod.

"Pleasure to meet you. Sorry it has to be under such circumstances." He extends a hand and I shake it as a few uncomfortable, furtive glances are exchanged around the table.

I look over the two agents and their assembled team. "Just trying to get a feel for the politics here. Who works for whom?"

Markinson clears his throat. "This is Agent Barbara Cardwell."

Caldwell shakes hands with me and Lori.

Markinson continues: "Agent Caldwell heads up the CARD team that's just joined us from D.C. Stands for Child Abduction Rapid Deployment team. They've come equipped with all this fancy gear to advise us and facilitate communications. These kind of cases are all they do."

An open laptop sits on the table next to Caldwell. She leans over it and taps a couple of keys. Instantly, a detailed, color-coded map of greater Richmond and the surrounding areas fills the screen. "This map gives us the big picture. We can zoom into more detailed grids to allow us to pinpoint all of the registered sex offenders in the region. It's much more comprehensive and up-to-date than the one available to private citizens." She runs a finger across the computer touchpad and taps another key.

A different screen pops up, this one filled with charts, menus, and smaller maps. "We've also established a complete communications command post. Basically, the idea is to monitor every contact with the kidnapper from as many different angles as possible: analyzing voice, incoming call data, and whatever other information we can gather. If the caller makes the mistake of using a cell phone, we can nail his location, give or take a few yards. The phone call that came in a little while ago originated from a pay phone at Potomac Mills shopping center up I-95 between Fredericksburg and Arlington, which makes things difficult because it's actually the biggest tourist destination in the state. There are just too many people. But we've got folks keeping an eye on things on the ground up there, just in case."

I clear my throat. "He won't use the same phone."

"We know. But he might just try another one in the area."

"You think he's taken Marnee somewhere up there then, Northern Virginia?"

"Not necessarily. The caller may have traveled up there to throw us off. When we asked where he wanted us to bring the money, he said it would be somewhere in Richmond."

She pauses. Eyes glance around the table.

Alex, who has been standing to one side, steps forward.

"Glad to see you up and around, Jerry. I'm thankful for your experience."

His voice carries the same weighty business manner he must use in the courtroom, but it's not really working here. I don't doubt he loves Marnee, as long it doesn't affect his lifestyle, but when it comes to me, his soon-to-be ex-father-in-law, I get the feeling he'd just as soon I hurry up and croak.

It was a disquieting scene back at the beach house with Alex and his half-dressed adulteress trying to awkwardly explain their secretive presence there while absorbing the news about Marnee.

I look again at Markinson. "You find out anything more about those boot prints?"

Markinson gives me a blank look, glances at Ford for help.

"Oh, yeah, right," Ford says. "The lab confirmed they were what you thought they were, some kind of common gardening boot. Problem is trying to narrow it down. Our best lead right now is they may have come from someone working on one of the homes under construction next door. We contacted the general contractor. They're sending a list of all the workers who had access to the site."

It makes perfect sense. That's what I'd be doing if it were my case.

"And if the construction workers all check out okay?"

"Then I guess we go back to square one."

Markinson interrupts. "We're all over this, Jerry. Every aspect. You don't need to worry."

I know when I'm being turfed.

"Anything else you'd like to ask us about?"

Should I give them the name Edgar remembered? Should I tell them about the Brentlou case and Rebecca and everything else that still haunts me? Maybe my obsession is creating connections where there are none. Maybe Marnee being missing has stirred up ghosts in me that will only slow them down.

"No. Nothing. Not right now."

"Good. Well, at least now we know there's an excellent chance Marnee's still alive. That's a whole lot better than the alternative."

I nod and everyone seems to join the chorus. But I can't shake the memories of so many dead bodies over the years. The discomfort in the room is almost palpable. The agents and Ford show respect, but they obviously want me out of their hair so they can continue their work.

Lori moves to my side.

"Why don't you and Colin head on upstairs where you can talk and rest?"

"I don't need to rest."

"Just sit and talk then."

Markinson's stare meets mine. There is genuine empathy in the agent's face, but the man's got a job to do.

Let them have their reign. I lower my gaze and nod my head.

120

Eighteen

"Dad?"

The knock at the door comes a few minutes later upstairs.

The spare bedroom is at the head of the stairs. I have slept here on a couple of occasions before. It is uniquely furnished in Lori's distinctive style. She likes to pick up funky antiques at rummage sales and she likes a lot of color. I lie on top of a green and maroon bedspread with yellow pillow shams.

I lift my head as Lori enters. "What's happening?"

"Nothing new. But Alex wants to talk with you."

"He does, huh?"

"Try to be civil."

"You want to come?"

"No. He said he wants to talk to you alone."

"You want me to punch him for you?"

"That's beside the point."

We look at one another for a moment. "Splendid. Where is he?"

"He's down in the den."

I sit up and swing my legs off the bed.

"Dad, you don't have to...I mean, I was going to ask him to come up here."

"I'd rather surprise him."

• • •

Until he moved out of the house, the den used to serve as Alex's private domain. A richly appointed home office, walls paneled in dark wood below a chair rail, is built around a cherry desk and matching bookshelves. An armoire cradles a flat screen TV flanked by a leather couch and wet bar. Long, draped windows look out on the back lawn.

Today the door stands open. Alex sits in the chair behind the desk typing feverishly on his laptop, for the moment at least doing a decent job of playing the broken man, his face haunted by the pale disbelief of one who is missing a child. He looks surprised when I knock on the doorframe.

"Jerry? Come on in. You didn't have to get out bed."

"I wanted to."

He stands momentarily from behind his desk as I sink into one of the collegiate side chairs facing him.

"Lori told me you wanted to talk with me."

"That's right." He moves back behind the desk and sits down. "I guess we're all still in a state of shock. It just doesn't seem real, all the people outside and the police and everything."

"No, it doesn't."

"You work any disappearances like this when you were on the job?"

"Only after the fact, I'm afraid." I scan the room for a moment. It's hard to keep looking at him without getting angry, without tasting the bitter bile of whatever well of resentment has been building up inside of me.

Our eyes finally meet again.

"The FBI wants us to come up with the money for the ransom," he says. "They say that's the best way to get Marnee back. Do you agree?"

I shrug. "They're the experts. I'm sure they've studied the odds. Can you and Lori raise the money?"

"If we cash in some retirement accounts."

"Is that all you wanted to talk to me about, the ransom?"

Alex manipulates something on his keyboard touchpad and lowers the lid on his laptop; it clicks shut with a snap. He leans back in his chair and folds his hands together on top of his stomach. "I know you don't like me much, Jerry. Especially considering what's going on between Lori and me."

I curl my mouth. Why deny it?

"I need to talk to you about something else though that has to do with Marnee. I'm not sure it's relevant." He stares as if attempting to gauge my response.

If he telegraphed the opening of his cross-examination any louder, I'd be struck deaf. "I'm all ears."

He sighs. "Apparently Marnee and Lori were having a conversation a few weeks ago about you and her grandmother."

"Rebecca."

"Yes."

"How come Lori never mentioned it?"

"She may not have thought it was important. She doesn't know what I know about what happened later."

"Go on."

"Marnee had apparently grown very curious about what happened to her grandmother, why she was incarcerated, whatever went on between the two of you."

"That's news to me. Although it seems pretty natural."

"Marnee never said anything to you about it?"

"No."

"I think she was actually afraid to ask you about it."

"Why? What do you mean?"

He shifts his expression as if deciding whether to go on before leaning forward, sliding his laptop out of the way, and placing his hands on the desk. "Do you remember Marnee and Lori visiting you at your house one day last month?"

"Sure. Lori comes by almost every day. And Marnee's been with her a few times."

"On one of her visits a couple of weeks ago Marnee must have left the room for a while. Do you remember that?"

"Not really, but it could have happened. Lori and I talk a lot. Sometimes she reads me poetry. Marnee usually runs off to the kitchen or watches a movie in the living room."

"How about the basement?"

"The basement?"

"Has Marnee ever been in your basement?"

I have to stop and think. It seems like an odd question in light of the fact Colin and I have just been down there. "Once or twice I suppose. It's mostly just old junk stored down there."

"But there's an old office in your basement too, isn't there? You used to use it back when you were on the job."

"Yes, but she couldn't have gotten in there because that door is always kept locked."

He pauses for a moment. "Not if you have a key."

I stare at him. "Are you saying Marnee somehow got hold of my key and snuck into my office?"

"Yes."

"Because she was curious about Rebecca."

"That's right."

"How'd she get the key?"

"She told me she took it from your key ring in your back entryway."

"I forgot I had that one."

"She said her mom told her you used to keep an office down there. She tried each of the keys on the ring until she found the one that fit."

Now that I think about it, it seems perfectly plausible. Maybe that's why I thought things in the file seemed a little out of place, like someone had disturbed them. I should have told Marnee more about her Grandmother Rebecca. It might have quenched her curiosity.

"What did she get into?"

"Apparently she found your file on the Brentlou case."

"All right. She wants to know more about what happened to Rebecca, that would be a good place to start. Did she take something?"

"What did you used to do down there in that office, Jerry? Didn't you have an office at the precinct?"

Since Alex ignored my question, I ignore his. "Did she take something from my basement office, Alex?"

"Yes," he says. "She did. She brought me an un-cashed check."

"An un-cashed check?"

"You don't remember putting it there?"

I shake my head.

Alex glares at me with an accusatory air.

"You're going to have to be a little more specific, Alex, because I have no idea what you're talking about."

He sighs. "Inside the file was a check made out to you in the amount of one hundred dollars along with a note."

"A hundred dollars?"

"Yeah."

"What did the note say?"

"For your trouble."

I still don't have a clue.

"Who was the check from?"

He hesitates for a moment. "A woman used to lived Southside. There was a name, address, and phone number on the check, but she's moved since then. You may not like it, but I decided to see if I could track her down, and I did. She's elderly, a little senile, lives now over in Glen Allen."

"What's her name?"

"Mary Harper."

I do my best to stare at him without blinking. "You did all this over some hundred dollar check?"

He rubs a hand through his thick hair. "Yeah, well. Like I said, she found it in the Brentlou file. And, I don't know, it just looked a little suspicious."

Or maybe you were looking for some kind of an edge in an upcoming divorce preceding, I think, but say nothing. "Is the woman's name familiar to you?"

I can't risk trusting him with the footprint lead. "Maybe. She was a minor subject we interviewed in the case, but it never went anywhere."

"Written on the memo line of the check was the word shirt."

I glance out the window as an old memory stirs. When Edgar and I interviewed Mary Harper at her house, she accidentally splattered some ink on my best shirt. It had been a gift from Rebecca. The inkbottle came from some kind of calligraphy Harper had been working on. I told her not to worry about it, but she sent the check anyway. It came several weeks later while we were trying to prepare for Rebecca's trial, and I must have just stashed it in the Brentlou file and forgotten about it.

"She spilled a little ink on my shirt during the interview. She sent me the check to replace the shirt, but I never cashed it."

"Yeah. That jives with what the woman told me, although she wasn't exactly clear about the circumstances. Like I said, she's not exactly with the program these days. Her brother was there, and it seemed like he had to help her decipher what happened."

"Okay, so what's the big deal? Why didn't you just come to me about Marnee getting into my files?"

Alex crosses his arms and leans back in his chair. "I'm sorry. I guess I figured you don't exactly look in the best of shape these days. I didn't want to bother you with it and Marnee was afraid you might be mad."

"Where's the check now?"

"I turned it over to the FBI. I told them everything I just told you about how Marnee found them."

"What did they say?"

"They said it probably doesn't mean anything."

"And you think it does?"

"I'm not sure what to think anymore. You still haven't answered my question. You had a desk downtown. What were you doing in your basement office all those years? Lori told me Rebecca spent a lot of time with you down there."

"That's none of your business."

"It is if it helps find Marnee."

I can't think of a good comeback. He either knows I'm avoiding telling the whole truth or thinks I just plain forgot, maybe in a moment of senility.

"What else did you talk to Mary Harper about?"

"Well, like I said, I didn't talk much with her directly. She seemed pretty confused. I heard back from her brother a couple of hours later and talked it through with him. He lives up near D.C. Retired from being pretty high up at the GSA. Says his sister has taken a turn for the worse mentally the past few months."

"Like Edgar."

"Who?"

"Never mind."

"Anyway, the brother seems like a decent sort, mostly concerned for his sister's well-being. Apparently he's making arrangements for her to move into an assisted care facility."

"You think Marnee was telling you the truth about how she came by the check?"

He rubs the bristle on his chin, deflated. "I don't see why or how she could have made up something like that. Like I said, she got scared, so she brought it to me."

"To you and not to her mother."

"She was afraid she might get in trouble with Lori for sneaking into your office."

"So if you've already given everything to the FBI, why talk to me about it? You asked me in here because you were thinking the check Marnee took from my office might have some other kind of connection to Marnee's disappearance I might be holding out on?"

"Basically." He leans back in his chair and runs his fingers through his hair. "I know it seems a little far-fetched. I've just been sitting here wracking my brain trying to come up with something, anything about Marnee that might help." He sighs. "I'm sorry, Jerry. I wasn't trying to suggest anything sinister on your part. I just don't get why anyone might have taken Marnee and be holding her for ransom."

"Me either." Nor do I get how such a familiar boot print ended up at the scene where Marnee was abducted.

"Oh, there was one other thing. The note the woman wrote? It was on the back of one of those old green kind of restaurant receipts with an order for a couple of orders of coffee, eggs, bacon, and toast. She must have just picked up some random piece of paper."

"What restaurant?"

"I tried to look it up but the place must have gone out of business long ago. It didn't seem to have a name really, but at the bottom you could see it was part of some motel called The Virginia Dixie Motor Court."

Nineteen

L ori meets me in the hallway on the way back upstairs.
She's come out of Marnee's room where I imagine she's
been looking around and praying and thinking who knows
what. It's hard not to stare at the tension constricting her
face.

"How'd the talk go?"

"Good."

"Anything I need to know?"

"Not really. Alex is just poking around in some things,
trying to figure out what might have happened to Marnee."

"Does he have any ideas?"

"A couple of old names maybe. We'll see."

She places a hand on my arm. "Did you forget about
your doctor's appointment this morning?"

"No, I didn't forget. I was just going to call and cancel."

At this point, it seems not only excessive but ridiculous.

"But you have to go, Dad. It's important they see you
every week at this stage, they said, so they can check your
blood levels and adjust your medications if necessary."

"I can't be bothered going to the doctor right now.
Not with Marnee missing."

"Do it for me then."

"You've already got enough to worry about."

"Exactly. Which is why I really want you to go."

I can see the value in this if it makes her feel better, but I still don't like the idea.

"What's happening downstairs?"

"Nothing," she says.

"How are you doing?"

"Hanging in there." She forces a grim smile but her expression betrays her. "At this point, what else can I do?"

"You let me know if you're not happy with the way they're handling things."

"All right."

"What Colin was talking about earlier—do you and Alex have access to the kind of money the kidnapper is demanding?"

"Alex is taking care of it. I'm not sure how and I don't really much care at this point."

"I've still got some money."

She holds up her hands. "Don't even think about it, Dad."

"You sure?"

"I'm sure."

Behind her, a photo of a smiling Marnee clings to the wall. When the weather was right, sometimes I would take her fishing in a neighbor's little boat on a nearby pond. Marnee loved every minute of it, never showed any squeamishness when it came to baiting the hook, but she always said a cute little prayer for both the worm and the fish before dropping her bait in the water. If it would help get her back safely, I'd almost be ready to borrow the money from the devil himself.

"Your appointment's in less than an hour, you know," she says. "Colin can drive you. Do you need directions?"

"Don't worry. I remember the way. Is Hal Ford still downstairs?"

"Yes, I think so." She gives me a curious look.

"I want to talk to him again before I go."

"Maybe you shouldn't. I overheard him talking with the FBI people about you. I told him you had a doctor's appointment and he said he thought it was a good idea for you to go."

"It gets me out of their hair, I suppose."

She says nothing, but gives my arm a squeeze.

Lori leaves to get Colin. A moment later, he comes bounding down the stairs. We use the back stairs and head out the door through the kitchen. Alex and Hal Ford and the FBI agents must all be meeting or doing something else out in the living room. Part of me wants to be in there with them, but another part of me realizes for what we need to do next, Colin and I will have to go it alone.

A uniformed cop is standing guard outside in the driveway. A young man who, if he's not a rookie must be very close to it, standing watch with piercing green eyes and a closely cropped haircut beneath the back of his official cap. Me, forty years ago.

Colin jumps in the car next to me. "Mom says she should be doing a better job of watching out for you right now, but she can't."

It doesn't surprise me, but I still hate hearing this. "I don't need watching out for."

He twists the steering wheel as we pull out onto River Road and the houses begin to speed by.

"Some people are always looking for something to feel guilty about, Colin. And that sometimes includes your Mother. It doesn't mean you have to feel guilty along with them."

"You think God let someone take Marnee, Granddad?"

"I don't think God ever wants a little girl to be kidnapped."

"Maybe Mom's right though. Maybe it's because I messed up. Marnee is going to die too and it'll be my fault."

"She's not going to die if any of us can help it, Colin.

And the person to blame is whoever took her. We all share responsibility for what happens to her now: you, your parents, the FBI. You can't just single yourself out. It's selfish to try to take responsibility alone. Took me a lot of years to understand that. Not that it makes it any easier."

"When we get her back, I mean, if we find her and everything, do you think she's going to be damaged, like in her mind and stuff?"

I don't want to delve into such things with Colin. Not yet. My job never entailed victim's counseling. We were about more measurable results: finding whomever turned them into victims in the first place. But I can't help picturing Marnee, wherever she is now, and the terror she must be experiencing.

"I don't know, Colin. We'll just have to wait and see."

He says nothing more.

A few minutes later, we arrive in front of the medical office complex adjacent to Henrico Doctors Hospital.

Colin starts to turn the wheel. "Which way do we go in?"

"We don't."

"What?"

"Keep going straight. We're not going to see the doctor right now."

❁

Twenty

*R*ebecca *was forty-four years old when she went to prison. At sentencing, the judge's instructions to the jury were specific: they were to disregard the potential guilt or innocence of her victim Jacob Gramm since he was never afforded the opportunity to stand trial himself, although they could make allowance for Rebecca's past. The jury gave her twenty years.*

It might as well have been twenty thousand as far as I was concerned. The Commonwealth shipped her off to serve her sentence at the Virginia Correctional Center for Women thirty miles outside Richmond.

At least the RPD job to which they'd demoted me afforded me Monday through Friday hours. I left our Richmond neighborhood every Saturday morning by seven AM because I wanted to be able to maximize my time with Rebecca. It was a pleasant enough drive West on route six to Goochland. In the summertime, I'd pass fishermen, their pickups parked in haphazard highway pull-offs as they worked the upstream stretches of the James. Often, Lori would come too, and in the late fall or winter we'd catch a fleeting glimpse of wild turkeys, fog rising around their bent black shapes at the edge of some frost coated field, or groups of white-tailed deer, moving like wary spirits among the trees. I couldn't help but envying them their freedom.

Not so the women in their bright orange jumpsuits at the

prison, brought out to meet their loved ones: husbands or boyfriends, parents, and children of all ages.

Right from the beginning, Rebecca seemed noticeably thinner to me. Her graying hair had been cut shorter and drawn back across her forehead. I would always ask her how she was feeling. Fine, she would say. Had she been ill? No, she would always assure me.

Prison seemed to bring out something very different in Rebecca. Everyone in the prison visiting room picked up on it. "Saint Rebecca" was what her fellow inmates took to calling her, sometimes with derision.

"It's a minefield in here," she told me in a quiet voice one Saturday.

"What do you mean? You've been attacked?"

"No. That's not what I'm talking about." She lowered her voice even further. "There are a lot of dark spirits lurking here."

I had no doubt about that. "What can I do?" I asked.

"Pray. Pray I'm protected."

Some kind of oppression in the place was obviously wearing her down.

Rebecca often told me I pressed too much. She'd say she heard it in my voice every time I came home from working a new case. Like a haggard, beaten-down athlete who has lost the rhythm and the flow of the game, charging forward nonetheless, I would keep going until she would sit me down in a chair and begin to rub my neck and shoulders. Now I couldn't help but wonder if she was doing the same.

An argument broke out across the room, between an inmate and a man who was visiting her. Their loud, angry words caromed off the walls, and the woman rose and from her chair and began punching at the man, until the guards intervened to separate them and escort them from the room. Rebecca and I stared wordlessly along with the rest of the inmates and visitors.

"You see what I mean?" she said.

It felt like there was an air of inevitability about what

was happening. After all, Rebecca had once reasoned, if all of human experience amounted to an unseen war between good and evil, between life and death, then murder was its most immediate and ongoing Armageddon. And an unsolved murder amounted to both justice and redemption denied, no less than a kind of eternal damnation. How many dark spirits of injustice, hatred, and purgatory were locked up in here?

Four years of weekly visits passed, each one a little harder than the last. Every week, Rebecca asked about what I was doing and how things were going for me on the job. "Great," I always said.

"Liar," she finally said to me one day. "You're not a paper pusher. When are you going to retire from the force?"

Then one Saturday I noticed Rebecca looking particularly pale.

I took both of her hands in mine. "Have you been sick?"

Her smile lacked its usual energy. "Haven't quite been feeling myself, lately. I'm so tired."

"Have you seen a doctor?"

"Yes," she said. "I'm sure it's just a touch of the flu or something. They want to send me down to MCV for some tests."

• • •

A half an hour later, we are parked at the curb on a leafy side street in the west end.

"We're on," Colin snaps his cell phone shut.

We may be searching for a needle in a haystack, but Colin has just finished talking with none other than Mary Harper. I needed him to make the call. The woman may not be in complete possession of her faculties, but there is still the chance she might remember me.

"What did she say?"

"She says I'm welcome to come by to talk with her."

Mary Harper lives alone. Her husband passed away five years ago. The Harpers have only one child, a daughter, Nancy, who lives in Japan. Mary Harper also has a brother,

Lassiter, the one whom Alex apparently spoke to the phone, who only recently retired from a long career in government service.

Colin has lied to Harper, telling her his mother used to go to school with her daughter. He is writing a history for the school's anniversary yearbook, he said, and, since he can't easily get in touch with Nancy, he wants to know if he can stop by to ask Mrs. Harper a few questions.

Colin seems excited by the subterfuge.

"You get any sense there might be anything wrong?"

"Nope."

"No hesitation at all?"

"Un-uh. She seemed glad about having company."

"You're sure she understood you?"

"Pretty sure."

We drive on in silence. The amazing thing is it took a only a few minutes online to get a pretty complete general history of the life of Mary Harper. Is everybody's vital information such an open book these days? Machines have become a bigger part of the investigative equation than the people themselves. What are all the professional gumshoes doing anymore except sitting in front of computer screens?

But Colin still looks anxious, peering at the street through swollen eyes. Hoarseness has crept into his voice. How much real sleep has he has gotten since Marnee disappeared? It can't be much.

"Great job, Colin."

"Thanks."

"You sure you're up to this?"

He nods. He's busy typing the directions into the GPS on his phone. "The phone says it will take us nineteen minutes to get there. How much longer do you think before Dad needs to deliver the ransom?"

"Unknown. But I doubt it will be too long. For all we know, the kidnapper may have already called back."

Fifteen minutes later, we are driving into Mary Harper's neighborhood, an aging subdivision of single story ranches and split-levels where the afternoon sun bakes the yellow white pavement. The area appears peaceful enough. Sprinklers fan sprays of water across lawns. Children race around on bikes and play games in cul-de-sacs.

Colin looks down the block. "She said hers is the house with the white Chevrolet parked in front."

"Okay." Though the chances seem remote, I have to consider the possibility we might be walking into a hazardous situation, both for us and for Marnee. "You make sure to keep your cell phone handy when you walk into the house."

"You got it."

"If anything goes bad, you call. If something just doesn't feel right, you call."

"Okay."

"If you're not out in fifteen minutes like we agreed, I'll be coming in behind you and calling for help."

"Right."

Earlier, we stopped at a store and picked up a new temporary mobile phone, which Colin has helped me activate and showed me how to use.

"There it is," he says.

I spot the Chevrolet at the same time he does, about four houses in front of us on our right.

"Don't take your foot off the gas. Let's do a drive-by first."

"Sure. No problem."

We glide past the house. Not too fast and not too slow. Nothing to call attention to ourselves.

Mary Harper's home is a plain, brick-and-frame rancher with a carport and flowers in need of weeding growing up front. Out back, a bass boat that looks like it hasn't been touched in years rests on blocks to one side in front of an old camping trailer. The Chevy sits under the carport. There is also a dark blue BMW with D.C. plates in the driveway.

The Beemer surprises me. "That doesn't look like an old woman's car."

"Her brother, you think?"

"Probably. Your father said he was concerned about his sister. Keep going slow so I can get the license number." There is an old ballpoint pen with a scrap of paper in the passenger door storage bin. I fish it out and begin to write down the letters and numbers on the plate.

"Why didn't he answer the phone when I called?"

"It's not his house, for one. Or maybe he was out at the store or something."

We've driven beyond the house, far enough away so as not to arouse suspicion, but close enough where I can still see the front door, the carport and most of the lawn clearly in my outside mirror.

"Pull over and park here."

Colin brings the car to a halt and I check out the situation in the mirror. Despite the extra car in the driveway, I don't see any sign of activity at the Harper house, either inside or out, and I didn't see any when we passed. No curtains pulled to one side to survey the traffic, no signs of disorder or any irregularities among the casual clutter of the yard or the carport. The lawn has been freshly mowed; a riding John Deere lawnmower is visible behind some trashcans with wet grass still stuck to its tires.

"What do you think?" Colin twists his head to peer back at the dwelling.

"That answers our question. The brother must have been out mowing the lawn when you called. Are you still up for this?"

"Yeah."

"Remember, it's a long shot. If you see anything awry, you get out of there on the double?"

"Absolutely. Right"

The plan calls for me to remain here and keep watch while Colin walks in. Once he gains entry, Colin will continue the ruse he's established, asking his questions while keeping his eyes open to see if he can spy any gardening boots.

I'm concerned about Mary Harper's mental state, but maybe having the son present will make things easier. If Colin does spot the boots, the tricky part will come when he tries to take things further by obtaining a soil sample from the bottom of one of them so we can have it tested against the soil back at the camp. I've given him a small plastic bag to carry in his pocket and use if he gets the chance.

"Leave the keys in the ignition just in case."

"Okay."

"Remember, you don't want to give away our position, so don't go directly to the house. Walk around the block and come in from the other direction."

"Okay."

"Same on the way back."

"Sure."

I pat him on the arm.

He is up and out of the car, closing the door behind him before I can blink. Very little traffic passes along the street, and there is not another pedestrian in sight, except for a lone mailman working his down the row of houses on the other side of the street. I sink deeper into the seat and keep my gaze fixed on the image in the mirror.

A couple of minutes later, Colin appears at the other end of the block and begins to make his way down the sidewalk. As he nears Mary Parker's house, a barking dog runs out from around back of the carport. It's a small white thing, a Pomeranian, I think. It leaps around in front of the BMW, looking angry and terrified at the same time.

Colin slows his pace, eventually coming to a halt. He bends down to greet the dog, which stops its barking and begins inching toward Colin with its tail wagging. After a few more seconds, Colin is getting the back of his hand licked.

The front door opens to reveal an older man with thinning gray hair wearing pale coveralls, lawn-cutting clothes. Colin smiles and waves. They exchange words for a moment, and Colin is apparently invited into the house.

He bounds up the steps and disappears inside, the screen door gliding shut behind him.

❀

Twenty-One

The doctor sat across the table from Rebecca and me, Rebecca in her prison garb and leg shackles, the two of us holding hands beneath the tabletop. The doctor's name was Hiranandani, spelled out in clear letters on her dark nametag. Coolly professional, her skin was olive brown, her eyes the color of coffee framed by wispy black hair, all of which seemed accentuated by her starched white coat.

"There is no easy way to tell you this," Dr. Hiranandani began.

Rebecca and I had been husband and wife for so long by then I sometimes found it impossible to distinguish between my own feelings and hers. I was scared. Was she scared? I remembered long nights back when were together—maybe after we'd fought about something—just holding her, the two of us alone in our bed.

"I've gone over the test results with the oncologist and the surgeon. Unfortunately, Mrs. Strickland, the cancer has spread. I'm afraid at this stage the chances of a cure are very slim."

I was supposed to be the one leading the charge to protect Rebecca. While that might seem an antiquated and out-of-fashion idea to some, there was comfort and, Rebecca always told me, an unusual liberation for her, in such an uncomplicated arrangement. But in the face of such odds, such chivalry seemed in vain.

Rebecca's hand pressed harder into mine.

"How much time do I have left?" she asked.

"That's difficult to say. Weeks, most likely. It might even be a couple of months. But based on your most recent series of tests, I'm not optimistic."

Given the difference in our years, I had always anticipated I would go before my bride. The medical details, as they were deciphered and discussed, hung in the air like sterile bits of cloth. I would still have many questions, of course, attempting to defeat the inevitable in my own way. In the end, it must have only come across as so much posturing. The physical particulars were less important than the currents of the moment anyway – spirits quickening, whispers and gestures of the mind and heart.

After finishing with the prognosis and asking if we had any final questions, Dr. Hiranandani, in a surprising gesture that pierced through her expert's decorum, reached her own hand across the table to us and offered to pray.

In later dreams, I would remember everything about those moments: the grasping of fingers, the cloak of calm that descended like an invisible tethered realm, the room and the hospital and the city fallen away. I could believe then there was a total new dimension just as Rebecca had always described, a country with streets of gold ahead of us.

When I awoke from what seemed to me a trance, Rebecca and the doctor were still there, but it was obvious Rebecca had already made her decision. I could see it in the resolute stillness of her eyes. Time to move on.

• • •

We agreed on fifteen minutes. Colin has already been in the house for seventeen. I have the new cell phone in my hand, and I'm about to call 911 when the front screen door pushes open again. Colin's blue-jean clad leg appears followed by the rest of him, moving out onto the front stoop. He is smiling and still talking with someone inside. After another minute he waves, turns, and steps down onto the sidewalk.

I breathe a sigh of relief.

Minutes later, seated next to me in the car, Colin wears an odd expression.

"That was weird."

"What do you mean?"

"I saw the boots. Big and green. They were just sitting on a mat by the refrigerator in the kitchen."

"Are they the kind we're looking for?"

"I think so. But the woman, Mrs. Harper, was really nice. She fed me milk and cookies. I almost felt bad about lying to her. What you said Dad told you was right though. She did seem a little bit loopy. She kept talking and talking and talking. It was all I could do to back out of there."

"Did she look feeble?"

"Not particularly. She looked okay for her age."

"You see any cuts and bruises on her face or hands?"

"Nope. Why?"

"If she took Marnee by force, Marnee would have fought back."

"What about the brother?"

"I met him for just a second. He said his name was Lassiter. Didn't say much else. I tried not to let on I knew anything about him."

"How old is he?"

"I don't know...your age, I guess? Maybe younger. He looked pretty serious."

"Did you talk much with him?"

"Not really. He said he had some things to take care of upstairs. I got the feeling he was packing his sister's stuff up for moving. I saw a bunch of boxes lying around."

"That jibes with what your dad was saying. What happened with the boots? Were you able to get us a sample?"

"No. That's what was weird. Mrs. Parker and I were still in the kitchen. The boots were on the floor right across from me. I was finishing up my cookie and she had turned to put the cookie jar back into her pantry. I bent over the boots and was just about to pull out the plastic bag when I heard footsteps from the living room and the brother was suddenly standing there in the doorway from the kitchen.

"Did he see you?"

"I don't know. I said something like 'nice boots, my mom used to have pair.'"

"Okay. What happened then?"

"He just nodded, but he didn't leave. He went to the refrigerator and pulled out a water bottle and an apple and stood there and started to eat it. That's when I told them thank you and I said I had to go."

"Good. You did the right thing."

"So what do we do now?"

I tilt my head to gaze into the rear view mirror at the house. "Good question. We don't have enough information to prove anything at this point, if there is even anything to prove. We may not have much time." I look at my watch, thinking about Alex and the conversation he supposedly had with the son.

"Maybe we should just tell the FBI what I saw and let them deal with it."

"Maybe. But they'll probably just push it down their list of things to follow up on. I know I would. Tell you what. Why don't we sit here and wait them out. See what develops."

"What, you mean like a stakeout?"

"Yeah. How's that sound?"

"Cool."

"Sooner or later, one of them will have to go out, and maybe they'll even leave together."

"Then we break in and get our boots."

"If it comes down to any breaking and entering, I'll be the one to go in. You can stand lookout, but if anybody asks, you didn't really know what I was up to."

"Sure." Colin doesn't seem too happy with the idea of letting his granddad do the dirty work, but he nods anyway. "How long do you think this might take?"

"No telling."

"What do we do if we have to go to the bathroom?"

"It's not very pretty. We used to always keep an empty Coke bottle handy."

Colin scans the back seat. The floor is littered with all sorts of smaller trash, but the best he can come up with is a dirty Styrofoam cup. "Will this work?"

"All right," I say. "We'll deal with peeing when we have to deal with it."

• • •

But as it turns out, there is no need. We've only been sitting for another ten minutes or so before Lassiter Harper walks out through the carport from somewhere behind the house. He looks like he's cleaned himself up. He is wearing a light sport coat over khaki slacks and carries a large black garbage bag by the top. A trash receptacle on wheels stands propped in front of the house at the curb. Harper lifts the lid and drops the bag inside. Then he turns and opens the door to his BMW.

He pauses for a few moments, looking up and down the street.

"Stay still."

"What's he doing?" Colin strains to make out the scene in his mirror.

I don't think Harper spots us.

His mind apparently made up, he hops into his car, starts the engine and drives off in the opposite direction.

"You see what I saw?" I stare into the mirror as the BMW rounds the corner out of sight.

"Yeah."

"Turn the car around. We need to move."

Colin starts the engine. "You want me to follow him?"

"Yes, but we need to hurry. I need you to grab whatever he dumped in that trash can first."

Colin NASCARs the Saab into a three point turn and we peel out after the BMW. In front of the house, he stops the car, jumps out, and snatches the bag from the can.

At the end of the street, trash bag in hand, we spy the Beemer again, stopped at a light on the busier entrance highway a couple of hundred yards in the distance.

"Not too fast now. Give him some space. All we need to do is keep him in sight. He's probably not expecting to be followed, but you never know."

My suspicions have been heightened after catching the bag Colin threw me across the seat. I undo the tie strip.

"Well, lookee here." Sure enough, inside is a brown paper bag and inside the second bag is a pair of oversized, dark green gardening boots.

"How'd you know it was the boots?"

"Lucky guess." I lift the top of the bag to look inside and examine the contents more closely. "There's a problem though. They're all wet. Looks like he's cleaned them off."

"So much for our soil sample."

"We'll see. We still have the prints." More questions come to my mind, but are they being answered fast enough to find out what exactly is happening with Mary and Lassiter Harper or make any difference for Marnee? Does chasing after Harper really have anything to do with what has happened to her?

"He's pulling away from the light. Should I stay with him?"

"Go for it." A thought burbles up from my subconscious—a crazy one, but it just might work. "I wonder how much he cares about his car?"

"What?"

"It's an expensive car."

"What you are saying, Granddad?"

The BMW is only four or five cars ahead of us a half-mile further down the road as we slow to a stop at the next light. There is a gas station and convenience store to our right. "Pull in here."

"What?"

"Quick, pull in."

Colin does as I instruct. He brings the Saab to a stop at the edge of the convenience store parking lot.

"What are we doing?"

"Hurry, you need to get out."

"Really? Why?"

"You can wait for me here. I'm going to drive."

Twenty-Two

I t's been a while since I've driven a car, but I haven't forgotten how. The Saab still has some pep in it. After almost losing him, I come within sight of Harper's BMW again when he is hung up at a light. I close the gap.

Colin objected to me driving, of course, but I gave him little choice in the matter.

I accelerate around a couple of slower moving cars and move into position directly behind the BMW. Harper doesn't seem to be paying me any mind. Perfect. Another traffic signal up ahead, a line of stopped cars, and his brake lights coming to life are the opportunity I've been waiting for.

I feather the brake and reduce my speed to keep things under control. The traffic light remains red.

In front of me, the BMW has slowed to a complete stop. As it does, I brake too, but not enough to bring the Saab to a halt. I glide into the back of the BMW at about five miles an hour.

A minor jolt shakes the Saab as I slam on my brakes. My airbag doesn't deploy, thankfully. Still, I engage in a little play-acting for effect by throwing my hands up in the air. I reach down and push the gearshift into park.

As I hoped, the collision has gotten Harper's attention. He adjusts his rearview mirror to take a look at me and turns on his flashers. Traffic backs up behind us. I power down my window, find the correct button on the Saab's dash, and turn on my flashers as well.

Harper climbs out of his car. He is tall, well over six feet, with a full head of gray hair and an angular face for his age camouflaged by stylish sunglasses, wearing brown loafers and an olive-colored polo shirt beneath his sport coat. He steps back to my driver side door with a stern expression.

"You hit the back of my car, sir."

I give him a sheepish grin. "I'm sorry. I must not have been paying attention."

He pulls off his sunglasses and blinks at me with piercing, dark brown eyes. "Are you all right?"

"Fine. I'm fine." I push open my own door and climb out. "Maybe we should call the police." Leaning against the hood, I edge around the front of the car to stand beside him.

Together we look at the front of the Saab, which doesn't appear to be any worse for the wear except for a bent front license plate. He turns to examine the back of his car, noting a scrape in the paint but no major structural damage. "I don't see any need for the police. We're both fine, and there doesn't appear to be any significant damage. Just a scrape."

"Are you sure? I have insurance."

"Absolutely." He looks me over for a moment. "It's okay. I'm late for a meeting."

Something about him fuels my anxiety. The jaws of darkness. A line, I remember, from *Midsummer Night's Dream*.

I wonder if I'm imagining things, but not wanting to call the police makes him all the more suspicious in my book. For all I know, he and his sister could have Marnee stashed somewhere back at the house. I glance into the back seat of the BMW—it's empty.

"Maybe you should pop the trunk," I suggest. "Sometimes there's hidden damage you can't see right away."

He stares at me for a moment. "All right."

He steps around to his open driver's door and pushes a button. The trunk pops up a crack. He walks back behind the car and lifts it all the way open, looks around inside with me glancing over his shoulder. The trunk is empty except for a dark suitcase.

"Looks a-okay."

"All right, I guess. But I'd still feel better if I at least paid for that paint damage on your bumper."

He slams the trunk door shut. "Don't worry about it. Like I said, it's minimal." He's in a hurry to get wherever he's going.

Cars are swerving around us into the opposite lane. If we stay here much longer, someone's going to report this and we'll attract police attention whether he wants it or not.

"Can I at least get your contact information, so I can send you some money or something?"

"No, no. Like I said, it's fine. Don't worry about it."

With a wave he climbs back into his car and closes the door, driving away into the stream of traffic as if the accident never occurred.

Twenty-Three

B ack at the convenience store, Colin crawls in behind
the wheel again.

"You bent the front license plate. What happened?"

I give him a brief rundown. We head back along the
street the way we've come. To be safe, we're going to have
to check out Mary Harper's place more thoroughly.

"This is crazy. You think the brother has something to
with what's happened to Marnee?"

"We should know soon enough."

Before we pull up in front of the sister's house again, I
call Ford with the license plate number from Harper's BMW.

"What's going on, Jerry? I thought you were supposed
to be at the doctor. Who is this guy in the car you're asking
about?"

I remind him of the connection to the boots.

"Just trust me on this one and have them run the plate,
will you? Find out everything you can."

"The Feds aren't going to like the sound of this. I'm
not sure I do."

"Hal, this is my granddaughter we're talking about.
The guy's acting squirrelly. I just want to follow up on this
lead."

"About some twenty-year-old footprints?"

"There's more to it than that. I'll explain more next
time we talk. Got to run."

• • •

At the Harper house, the little dog is barking maniacally again. I instruct Colin to park a couple of houses away.

"What do you want to do?" He looks ready to storm the place.

This isn't exactly what I have in mind.

"I want you to knock on the door, go in, and talk with her like you did before. Tell her you were nervous the first time, this is your first interview for your project, and you forgot a couple of the most important questions. Make something up."

"All right. I can do that. She'll probably just start talking again."

"Exactly what I'm counting on. But the most important thing I want you to do is to stand or sit between her and the far side of the house. Keep her looking that way. I'm going to walk in through the carport and slip around back."

"What about the dog?"

"Ask her to let him outside. I think I know how to take care of the little tyke."

"How are you going to get into the house?"

"If you can keep her up front in the living room, I'm hoping to just walk in through the back door."

"What if it's locked?"

"You let me worry about that."

"All right. What then?"

"I'll do a sweep of the house checking for Marnee. Could you tell if they have a basement?"

He shakes his head. "I'm not sure."

"All right. I'll check it out."

"What if you find something?"

"I think the two of us can overpower an old lady, don't you? Then we can call in the cavalry."

"Got it."

I wait until he has knocked on the door and gone inside again before stepping out of the car. As if on cue, the dog starts barking inside the house. Outside it remains mostly quiet except for the distant sound of a leaf blower a couple of blocks away. Turning up the driveway, I get a view in through the picture window of Colin standing and talking with the old woman. Sure enough, she's turned away from me. I make my way through the carport and around back, shielding myself from view as best I can against the building, but the walls must be thin because the dog is going ballistic.

A few seconds later the woman pushes the back screen door open.

"You get out to run in the grass. Go on now. Get out, you."

The dog, still barking, rushes out. He turns straight at me.

But I am ready for him. The wrapper from an old, half-eaten taco I've rescued from the floor of Colin's car rests in my hand along with an old taco-juice-stained shoelace lying next to it. I hope whatever microbes might be infesting the things won't make the creature sick. I bend down on one knee to show him I'm no threat and hold out the morsel. His nose takes over his brain and before you know it, he is sniffing the wrapper and I am cradling him in one arm.

I walk him over to the camper and try the door. The handle sticks at first, but I manage to pry it open with a pop. A musty odor wafts out. Inside, there is nothing but an empty table and a bench.

I deposit the dog, now perfectly happy with his newfound treasure, on the bench, and shut the trailer door.

Returning to the house, the back screen door swings silently open in my hands. From the front room, the woman's voice prattles on. Colin is doing his job.

I start clearing the place, not knowing what to expect as I begin checking doors and closets. Thankfully, the house isn't big. There are only a couple of bedrooms.

I find nothing there. The same goes for the rest of the house. Strangely enough, I find no evidence the brother is staying here either—no suitcase, no shaving kit, not even an extra toothbrush in the bathroom.

I manage to slip back out of the house as quietly as I came in, free the dog, who's now my best friend, and make my way back to Colin's car, signaling him through the picture window to wrap things up as I pass by.

A few minutes later, we are driving away down the street.

"Find anything?"

I shake my head. "Nothing. Nothing at all. That lady keeps a tidy house."

"So maybe the boots don't mean anything."

I reach down and pick up the garbage bag and peer inside at them again. "They mean something."

Colin's cell phone goes off in his pocket. He reaches for it.

"Give it to me," I tell him. "You need to keep your attention on your driving."

He fishes out the device and points to the button for me to answer, which I do.

"Jerry? Is that you?" Hal Ford's voice booms through the handset.

"Right. I'm still with Colin."

"Good. We need both of you back here pronto to be with your daughter."

"Lori? Why?"

"Something arrived in the mail—Fedex, actually. It was placed in a drop box north of Richmond before the final pickup last night and delivered here to the house."

"What is it?"

The line stays silent a moment. Hal doesn't normally beat around the bush. "It's a little girl's toe," he says.

Twenty-Four

L ori sits alone at her kitchen table. Untouched on the cloth placemat in front of her is a cup of herbal tea and an open, half-empty box of tea bags. She looks like a war victim, consumed by the type of vacant stare you see in pictures of far off places on the television.

"You okay?"

We make eye contact. Colin and I have just come in through the back door.

She shakes her head slowly and fixes her gaze on mine. "She'll never dance," she says.

"I know." I bend over and cradle her head in my arms as she starts to cry. "I know."

Her tear-filled gaze rises to meet mine a second time, but now it is as if she is looking through me to some far off, dangerous place.

Colin kneels next to her and places a hand on her shoulder. Lori looks down at the table again, cupping one hand to her forehead to shield her eyes. She shudders a little as she sobs.

From the front of the house, I sense an increased urgency among the FBI agents and police. The sound of tense, muted conversation filters back to us through the dining room. After a minute, Lori's breathing slows, and I step back as she manages to get her tears in check.

"I'm sorry we weren't here when the package came," I say.

"You should be." She faces me once more. "It doesn't make me very happy. You were supposed to be seeing the doctor. The office even called."

"We were out in Glen Allen."

"The FBI people said you might be making them waste their resources, or even endangering Marnee. Why can't you just do what you're supposed to for once?"

I don't quite know how to answer her, so I say nothing.

Out the window, Hal Ford leans against the hood of his car, talking on the phone. Two additional government sedans are parked behind him on the lawn.

"Wait just one minute, please." I try to keep my voice gentle. "I need to talk to Hal. You stay here with Colin."

Outside, my arms and legs move too slowly—they seem to belong to someone else. Hal Ford is still speaking into his cell phone. Glancing up to see me coming, he ends his conversation, pushes a button on the phone, and sticks it back in his pocket.

"Hey, Jerry."

I search his eyes for answers. "What's going on?"

"You and your grandson have kicked up a crap storm, that's what. The AIC's been reaming up one side and down the other."

"They signed you up to be my babysitter."

"Something like that."

"I told you I wanted more information on those footprints."

"I hear what you're saying, but some senile old lady and her brother acting weirdly is hardly—"

"The FBI's talked to you about it then?"

"Yes."

"About what my son-in-law told them?"

"Yes."

"They're ignoring a potentially important piece of evidence, Hal. There's more here than meets the eye. Something started after Marnee took that stuff out of my office. It's too big a coincidence to ignore."

"The Feds don't think so."

"Well, maybe they should."

We stare at one another for a moment. I feel bad for snapping at an old friend, but there it is.

"What's the deal with the toe?"

"Whoever did it knew what they were doing, apparently. Almost a surgical cut. Came wrapped in gauze and sealed in a plastic bag.

"Doctor maybe?"

"Maybe. But it could be anyone with medical experience, like on a battlefield or something, even a paramedic."

"How do you know for sure the toe is Marnee's?"

"There was a note from the kidnapper attached, and the toenail had pink polish on it. Your daughter said Marnee wasn't wearing nail polish or anything of the sort when she left the house this morning. But we started calling around to some of the counselors and a couple of the other campers. One of them told us the counselors brought in a makeup kit yesterday, and some of the girls got together to paint nails for fun. The girl who was doing the painting says she remembers painting Marnee's pink."

Toenail polish. A rite of passage for a little girl.

"What did the note say?"

Hal frowns. "Basically, that if Lori and your son-in-law don't hurry up and cough up the ransom, there will be bigger body parts."

"Have they gotten the money together?"

"I think so. Your son-in-law's apparently working on that one."

"Has a meet been arranged?"

"Yeah. Tonight."

"Where?"

"East side. The State Fairgrounds off of Laburnum. There's a big Mid-Atlantic boat show going on there tomorrow. The note says they want your son-in-law to come alone."

"If the guy's coming down from D.C. way, that's not too far from I-95."

"We'll be watching all the access routes."

"No luck tracing him up North?"

"Nothing so far."

"You really think this is just about money, Hal?"

He shrugs. "Maybe not, but my opinion doesn't count for a whole lot at this point. Not on a case like this."

I don't know what to say to that. We both know he's right.

"Sorry, Jer. Wish I had better news."

"What about the prints and the boots?"

"You don't give up, do you?"

"Never been known to."

He looks at me for a moment. "Where are the boots now?"

"Colin has them in a plastic trash bag."

"Great." He smirks and shakes his head. "Tell that to a judge and jury...if there's ever a trial, the defense will get them thrown out."

I stare at him.

"All right. We'll have a look at them, but just because it's you, Jerry."

"You get any more info on the plate number I gave you?"

"Nothing yet on the plates. Feds don't seem very interested in that either."

The afternoon light is waning. The cell phone burbles in his hand and he turns away from me to talk to someone else.

Back in the darkening kitchen, light emanates from a small bulb under the range hood. Lori has her head down on the table, her hair a tangled mess, her face buried in her hands. Colin still stands over her with his arm around her shoulder. Lori looks up at me with swollen eyes.

"What did he say?"

"He filled me in about the toe."

"What does it mean?"

"I don't know," I tell her. "Maybe the FBI profilers have some clue. At least we know she's probably alive. The kidnapper's proven he has her."

"Because he wants the money."

"Yes. And also partly to taunt us."

Which is what worries me most. It's this latter element that might get Marnee killed. Does the sender's hubris stem from desperation, psychotic tendencies or worse? I can't say I saw any evidence of such behavior in my brief encounter with Lassiter Harper, or in what Colin told me about his sister, but you never know.

I talk about these issues from time to time with my students. Despite all the theories from forensic psychologists and the like, criminals keep coming along to reshape the mold. This is where things can grow numbingly complex, sorting among the savage possibilities, the ragged edge of a frustration so deep it seems beyond human understanding. Apparently, the bad guys aren't reading textbooks.

Lori's eyes darken. "I feel like this whole thing is like a boomerang to our past."

"Maybe. I don't know," I tell her. "I wish I did, sweetie. I just don't know."

"Everyone here seems to have switched gears since the envelope arrived."

I nod. "Makes the whole situation more delicate for them. If the kidnapper is communicating actively with us, it must mean he is in some sort of state of heightened anxiety, provoked either by talking with us or by his own actions."

"Actions. What kind of actions?"

I stare at her, thinking back to all the cases I'd worked over the years and the gray-haired old man whose car I'd just rammed.

Lori stands from the table. "You mean killing Marnee, don't you?"

I nod.

A switch seems to trip in her mind. "Tell me honestly. You think the FBI is capable of getting Marnee back alive?"

"I think they're the best at what they do. I think they're pulling out all the stops."

"That's not what I asked you."

"I know."

She searches my face. "Why are you so obsessed with chasing down these footprints, or whatever it is they are?"

I hesitate. With everything else she is facing, is now the time to burden Lori with trying to understand the truth about her Mother and me? "That's a long story...one I don't know if I have time, or even if I'm ready, to tell."

We stare at each other for a moment or two. She glances over at Colin before looking back to me.

"It has to do with Mom, doesn't it?"

"That's right." Maybe she already knows some of it.

"It has to do with the two of you, and why she shot the man she went to prison for killing."

"Potentially."

"Okay. Then we have to try to find Marnee ourselves."

"Exactly what I've been thinking."

"And you'll tell me everything when all this is over, about you and Mom, I mean."

"Already written it down."

"Good. What can I do to help?"

I shake my head. "Nothing's guaranteed."

"I'm not asking for guarantees. Doing anything beats sitting around here dying by degrees."

"All right then. Something strange is going on with these Harper folks in Glen Allen. We need to go back out to the house and keep an eye on them."

Lori gives me a quizzical look. "But what are we supposed to do exactly?"

"For now, keep a close eye on them. Sit on the house. Keep watch from down the street."

"That's it? Just sit there? Shouldn't we be trying to arrest them or something?"

"On what charge? Throwing away a pair of boots?"

"Could Marnee be at this house?"

"No. Colin and I cleared the place. She's not there."

She nods her head. "Okay. But it doesn't take all three of us to just and watch."

"No. I guess it doesn't."

"What's the address?"

"Colin has it on his phone GPS."

"I'll go."

"What?" Colin throws up his hands. "Mom, you can't—"

"Why not? I've got a cell phone and if I see anything I can call you. Alex is dealing with the ransom. You guys can keep doing whatever it is you've been doing. Maybe try to figure out where this man in the BMW went."

I'm torn, but what Lori says makes sense. "You sure about this?"

"I'm sure."

"I agree. I think it's a good idea, Colin. It frees us up."

Lori wipes away a sniffle with the back of her hand. "Thank you for being honest with me about Marnee."

"It's the least I owe you."

She takes me by the hand.

"Where are you and Colin heading?"

"Where's Alex?"

"He just left with a couple of agents. I think to go back to his condo."

"Then that's where we'll be," I say.

❁

Twenty-Five

*R*ebecca and I were married in her father's church. There
must have been more than three hundred family and friends
who attended what could only have been described as an
elaborate affair. Rebecca wouldn't have gone in for all the fuss
and neither would I, but her mom was all about the gaudy
wedding. For the remainder of her life Rebecca's mother, always
the picture of decorum and grace, seemed to have to work at
stifling her disappointment over her only daughter marrying a
cop.

My favorite example of this sideshow occurred during the
reception following the wedding. Like the wedding, it was a
gala affair with a live band playing swing and show tunes in
the ballroom of an exclusive private club near the University
of Richmond.

At the time, Edgar and I had only been partners about a
year, but I'd already learned to be wary of his occasional pranks.
The reception went off without a hitch until Rebecca and I cut
the wedding cake. As we held the knife together and began to
slice into the body of the cake, little did we expect to hit
something solid buried among the summer yellow sponge cake
and butter cream icing—like a pretend plastic police revolver.

I immediately looked over at Edgar and a table full of my
cop buddies, who burst out laughing as they watched us struggle
with the knife. When I exposed the toy gun, they stood and

raised their glasses in a cop salute to the bride and groom. Most everyone at the wedding took it in good humor, applauded, and joined in the toast. But the petrified look on Rebecca's mother's face was beyond priceless.

Years later, Rebecca and I remembered this incident with a laugh while the first smells of spring wafted into her hospital room. We all knew she didn't have much time left. She was painfully thin and her unseeing eyes had sunk deeper into their sockets. Still smiling, she asked me for a drink. I picked up the plastic cup of ginger ale and ice on her bed stand and held it up to her mouth, so she could drink it with a straw.

She reached out and took my hand. "Jerry, I want you to promise me something."

"Of course."

"If there's another woman out there after I'm gone. I mean, if you meet someone, if you fall in love again, I want you to be happy."

I couldn't speak.

She ran her hands along my arms, up and across my shoulders to my face, where they stroked my cheek, brushing away a tear.

But a small piece of that tear still fell on the specially made pillow supporting Rebecca's head, staining one of her favorite satin shams. She always loved the feel of the slick, silky material against her skin. It added a touch of romance to our marriage bed, she always said, and despite the modesty of living on a cop's salary, satin sheets, pillowcases, and throws were the one luxury she always insisted we have. The nursing staff had allowed us to fit her favorite set to her hospital bed.

Less than three days later, Rebecca insisted I go home one evening to rest. She actually looked a little better, her face a little brighter. She'd see me in the morning, she said, so I went home to catch a few hours of much-needed sleep.

But when I arrived back at the hospital just before the shift change the following morning, the head nurse stopped me

*in the hallway. She was just about to call me, she said. She was
so terribly sorry, they discovered Rebecca passed away peacefully
in the night.*

*Had Rebecca somehow known? Had she wanted to spare
me the very end?*

*The sheets would never be used again. They came to
represent everything I lost with Rebecca's death.*

*Not just the romance. Not just the thousands of times she
lay with me as my wife: keeper of the gorgeous voice, Harley
Davidson fanatic, fearless seeker of truth. Those sheets came to
represent the ease with which Rebecca slipped, finally and
inexorably, out of them, leaving me forever straining to catch
up.*

So much for satin.

• • •

Alex's SUV is parked outside his condo in the bright
midday light. An unmarked sedan sits beside it with two
federal agents inside.

"Looks like we got lucky." Colin wheels the Saab down
the row of cars looking for a free parking slot. "Unless the
FBI doesn't want Dad talking to us."

"Only one way to find out."

We locate a parking spot several condos away. The heat
is almost as oppressive as the day before as we approach the
front of Alex's place. The agents sit in their car with the
engine running with the A/C on. They have yet to note
our presence.

"We could try going in another way. There's a door
around back by the garage."

"You mean pull an end run."

"Whatever."

"Just might work. If there are more agents inside, at
least we'll have made it past the first line of defense."

We retrace our steps down the sidewalk and find our
way around back. A row of single garages flanks the
individual condos.

"Dad usually parks out front, except at night," Colin explains.

We locate the back of his unit and find a solid metal door with a small window toward the top and doorbell beside it. We ring the bell and wait thirty seconds. Nothing.

"Try it again."

Colin pushes the button. A chime sounds again through the door, so it's definitely working.

After a few more seconds, a chain scratches against the door from inside. The lock clicks and it swings open. Alex stands in the back entryway, yawning. He looks like he just got out of bed and is holding a portable phone to his ear. He motions us inside.

"Yeah," Alex says, turning his back to us and rejoining his conversation. "I hear you."

We follow him down a tiled hallway past a small bathroom and a den and then into the pushily decorated living room. I can almost feel my toes sink through my shoes into the carpet. Alex has moved off to the kitchen area, apparently in need of more privacy with his conversation.

"Nice place, huh?" Colin says.

I nod, thinking big criminal money.

But maybe that's just me being an old cop. Maybe I shouldn't be so judgmental. Maybe, if this guy weren't about to divorce my daughter, we could even be friends. Alex sent me a polite note a few weeks back when I received word about my prognosis. I have to give my son-in-law that. I probably should have responded, but I never wrote back.

"You want to sit down?" Colin points me toward a rich black leather sofa group that looks like it came right out of some custom designer's showroom.

"No, thanks. I'd rather stand."

"You all right?"

"Just tired, that's all." Tired and cranky.

Alex finishes his conversation in the other room and returns to join us. I look him over. He is wearing flip-flops and an old Washington Redskins jersey over his pajama bottoms.

"You napping, Alex?"

"Yeah. Sorry, fellas. That was the FBI. The agents out front and I are heading by the bank and my brokers office in an hour. I guess pulling together a half million in traceable cash will get you that kind of attention."

"They're not telling Colin and me anything. Any more word from the kidnapper?"

"No," he says. "Not exactly."

"What's that supposed to mean?"

"I don't know, Jerry. It's complicated. At this point, I really don't know." Alex sighs, rubbing at the stubble on his chin.

"You don't know."

"You guys come up with anything that might help?"

"Yes, we have. One gigantic coincidence concerning Marnee's breaking into my home office you just so happened to talk to me about."

"Yeah, the Feds filled me in. Something about some boots? But they said they didn't think it was going anywhere."

"Maybe. You mind if I ask why you aren't staying back at the house with Lori?"

"Like I said, the half million."

"Do Marnee's kidnapping and this ransom demand have to do with one of your crooked clients?"

"Nope." Alex hesitates. "Is that what you've been thinking, Jerry?" He glances across the room at Colin. "That just because of some of the work I do...."

"That's what I've been thinking." I follow his gaze.

Colin, who's been sitting on the leather sofa, pushes off his seat and rises to cross the room and join us. "I told you, Granddad, Dad wouldn't ever do anything to hurt Marnee or any of us."

"Of course," I say. "Maybe not on purpose, but—"

"Not even by accident," Alex says. "I've always gone to great pains to insulate my family from what I do. I have cops watching almost everything I do. I hire private investigators, security, you name it."

"PIs to provide protection for you? Is that it?"

"Something like that. Cop protection from an old pro. You ought to know how the game goes, Jerry."

How the game goes. I guess I know enough.

"You should be back home yourself, Jerry. Getting some rest. We've got a big night coming up. Hopefully between the police and the FBI, this will all be over in a few hours."

Something tells me this is not the whole truth. "Where's the ransom money coming from?"

"I have a couple of off-shore accounts."

"Off-shore accounts. Oh, that's just beautiful, Alex. What are you, laundering money for some of your drug kingpins now?"

"Many of my clients have legitimate financial considerations."

"Sure. Legitimate considerations. Like how to avoid paying all their taxes."

"It's all legal."

"Of course."

"Jerry, if this is about what's happening between Lori and me, we don't have time for this right now." He moves to place his hand reassuringly on my arm, like someone comforting an elderly person whom they consider not in complete possession of their faculties.

I push the hand away. "What are you up to, Alex?"

He steps back, looking hurt by my failure to accept his peaceful gesture. "What do you mean?"

"There's more going on here. I want to know exactly

what you know about Marnee and where she is. I want to
know exactly what you were just talking to the FBI about."

Alex looks down at the floor, says nothing.

"You're not going to tell me, are you?"

"You should go, Jerry. You and Colin should just go."

"You're not going to tell me and you're not going to
tell your son either because you're dirty."

He raises his head and our eyes meet, but all I'm looking
at is a blank stare.

"C'mon, Granddad. Let's just get out of here." Colin
reaches to take hold of my arm, and we turn to leave while
Alex watches us, his gaze eventually dropping away.

Twenty-Six

Late afternoon back in my own house. I awaken shivering beneath the blankets with spittle caking my lips. My throat feels parched and dry. The central air conditioning is still running full blast, a concession I've made to Colin, who is asleep in the spare bedroom down the hall. Sunlight filters through the window. The house is bathed in shadows and still.

Checking in with Lori before falling asleep, she said everything was quiet out in Glen Allen. No sign of activity at the Harper house. Don't worry, Dad, she said, get some rest—only a few more hours until the ransom exchange.

Time means little to me now. Time is what separates me from finding Marnee, separates me from my past. I want to believe Marnee is still alive, want it with every fiber of my being, but I wanted Rebecca to live, too. I am suddenly hungry, but I won't eat anything. I am fasting. Rebecca used to fast sometimes when she prayed.

I pull back the covers and slide out of bed. Maybe I'll go downstairs and get a glass of cold water and do some thinking. I reach for my robe as my feet hit the cool floor.

Down in the kitchen, the only sound comes from the refrigerator motor purring and the faint afternoon din of the city outside. I pick out some ice cubes from the freezer and dump them in a tall glass, then pour some water over them. The cubes crackle and crack. The sound is good. I sit down at the kitchen table, waiting for the water to get good and cold.

I decide my next move will be to awaken Colin and go relieve Lori out in Glen Allen. If we haven't found out anything more by the ransom deadline, what more is there to do?

Maybe I've been missing some speck of information from my basement office. Maybe Marnee saw some other things she wasn't supposed to see. I take a sip of the cool water, push to my feet leaving the glass on the table, and head to the basement door.

Switching on the stairwell light, I look down into the dim cavern of the level below. Should I wake up Colin to come help me look? No, the boy needs his sleep. I grab the railing and start down the stairs.

Cautiously, at first—I am thinking about what might be gnawing at my memory, what possibilities I might discover hidden among the files. There were a lot of threads to the Brentlou case. There is more to read in the file.

Almost to the bottom, my foot catches on the final step.

It is not a major stumble at first, just a momentary lack of balance, and I correct by bracing myself against the railing and wall. But as I do, my hand jams the bottom bracket in the railing, and before I realize what is happening I completely lose my equilibrium, falling, rolling through empty space for what seems like a miniature eternity, before bouncing off the landing and coming to rest at the base of the stairs.

My heart races out of control. There is pain my chest. I lie flat on my back, disoriented, as if in a dream.

All right, you old fool. When I finally recover my senses, I take assessment. There is no blood as far as I can see, and nothing feels broken, so that's good. I somehow seem to have landed with a skillful roll, like the eighteen-year-old football player I once was. Miraculous or lucky.

That's when I notice the lights are all on further into the basement. The door to my old office hangs open. Has Colin been down here?

Can't be. I just passed his lightly snoring form in the guest room on my way downstairs. My old .38 Police Special sits in a locked bedroom drawer. I consider heading back up the stairs after it.

"Jerry?"

The voice calls out from inside the office, but it hits me like a bolt from another dimension. I shake my head and put a hand to my ear. Maybe I hit the old noggin harder than I realized.

"Jerry?" Is that you?"

I must be hallucinating.

The voice, after all, is my Rebecca's, sounding alive and well.

Twenty-Seven

She is seated in the chair in front of the infamous wall of photos where I have seen her sitting and praying hundreds of times before. Pictures of the dead, whom she has prayed for and loved. She looks older, as you might expect, her hair not quite as lustrous as it used to be, her skin a bit more wrinkled, but her eyes still sparkle as they always did. There is no mistaking her retained beauty. She seems to have aged better than I, and the sight of her leaves me speechless.

"I thought it might be you."

"Rebecca?"

"Of course. Who did you expect would be down here at this hour of the night?"

"I can't believe it's you." I look down at my hands. Still the same brown spots, still the same seventy-year-old bones. "This must be some kind of a dream." I move closer, thinking maybe she'll dissolve, or float away like some apparition, but she stays firmly rooted to her chair.

"No dream. I've missed you, Jerry. I've missed you so much."

"But how? This is impossible. You, you're—"

"Dead?"

I nod.

"We'll have a lot to talk about, a lot to catch up on when the time comes. But that's not why I'm here."

I want to reach out and touch her. I want to take her and hold her in my arms again, but something causes me to hold back.

"I can't. I don't know what to do." I feel like I'm babbling to a ghost.

"I know. But Marnee's still missing. We don't have much time."

"But I just can't believe you're here. How—?"

"Shhh." She puts a finger to her lips. "If there's one thing I wish you'd have begun to listen to me about, Jerry Strickland, not just with your mind but with your heart, it's that there are a few things none us can ever know."

"Are you...are you real?"

She smiles the way a teacher might when speaking to a slow student. We stare at one another for a long moment until her face softens. "You don't need to understand that just yet."

"I still don't understand."

"But how can you be here?"

"How could I not be here?" She smiles some more, a different smile this time. I have almost forgotten how intoxicating her smile was, how I walked into the precinct one afternoon to catcalls and whistles when word got out about our engagement.

"You're here to help us find Marnee."

"Of course."

"Can you help?"

"I can pray," she says. "I'm here praying now."

My stomach seems to roll into my throat as I look past her at the murder photos. "But Marnee's not up there. Marnee's picture's not up there on the wall."

"You're right," she says. "It's not."

"Are you trying to tell me she's still alive?"

"I'm just here to help you, darling, like always. I'm afraid you're going to have to figure out the rest for yourself."

I've run out of questions because there are too many to ask all at once. It feels like time itself has sunk into a shallow standing, past and present colliding. All I know is a part of me feels like I am young again and I never want it to end. I move closer to her. I've got to touch her. She almost seems to be egging me on.

But at the last moment before my hand can reach out to feel her shoulder, her eyes dart back and forth between the door and me.

"Granddad?" Colin's voice rings down the stairwell from the kitchen above.

I turn back to look at the hallway. I can't wait to introduce Colin to his grandmother. I can't wait to see the expression on his face. But I seem to lose my equilibrium again for a moment. Before I realize what is happening, Colin is standing beside me.

How did he move so fast? I see the smear of blood on the doorjamb and feel the gash at the base of my scalp, warmth trickling down my forehead. I look at my fingers coated in blood.

"Granddad. Did you fall? Are you okay?"

"I'm fine, buddy. Really. It's okay."

"What are you doing down here?"

"Colin, I want to—" I turn back to introduce him to Rebecca, but she is gone.

Twenty-Eight

If there is one thing Lassiter Harper has always prided himself on it's his ability to manipulate a system. He's always had a sixth sense when it comes to people.

The government is a system. Big corporations are systems. Even churches are systems, the big ones anyway. At one time or another he's been able to work them all for his benefit. It's a pretty sweet irony, really. You keep your head down, do just enough work to keep the wheels greased, and don't call too much attention to yourself, and you'll usually get what you want in the end. Either that or you find a way to get it.

But sometimes systems break down. Sometimes, no matter how well you've poked and prodded and pulled the right strings, facts come back to haunt you. Or curious little girls, or feeble sisters. The darkness closing in around him seems to be growing stronger.

He reaches for his mobile phone and speed dials Mary's number. The phone rings several times before she finally picks up.

"Is it you?" Her voice sounds anxious. "Where are you?"

"On my way back down there. Don't worry, I'll be there in a little while."

"What day is it?"

"It's a Tuesday, and yesterday was Monday, but don't you worry about that."

"All right."

He breaks the connection and focuses again on the road.

It's sad. She is really going downhill, and though he eats a good diet and keeps himself in decent condition, he worries one day he will end up just like her. It was a stroke of good fortune she kept those old boots, and he still thinks it was a good idea cramming his feet into them again to throw off any investigators. But he wonders who that nosy kid was at the house, and he doesn't like having to involve Mary in his business. Even worse, how he is going to deal with her if she gets out of hand?

• • •

Climbing the stairs from the basement with Colin, a wave of weariness squeezes my chest like a malevolent hand. Fatigue from lack of sleep, or something more? I remember a guy on the force years ago who went out with one big cardiac explosion. A second or two of crushing pressure and pain and it must have been all over for him.

"Are you okay, Granddad? You like you've seen a ghost."

Maybe I have. For the first time in years, I feel the craving for cigarette. "Where's my gum?"

"I think I saw some on your dresser in the bedroom."

The kitchen phone rings just as we make it back upstairs. Thinking it must be Lori, I ask Colin to give me the handset.

"Hello, Jerry Strickland speaking." The words sound dry and distracted, even to me.

"Jerry?" The voice on the other end jogs an old circuit in my memory. There was a time, back in the day, when Edgar and I counted David Wilhelm among our close circle of friends. Young, hip, and at times a bit too self-important for his own good, David worked the crime beat for the Times-Dispatch. He was one of the few print journalists who wrote about the Jacob Gramm shooting and Rebecca's trial in an even-handed way.

Through the years, David and I have kept in touch. Since leaving the Times- Dispatch, he moved on to become editor-in-chief of one of those weekly newspapers that used to be called 'alternative' but now seem the opposite, the kind that mixes liberal political writing with funky movie and music reviews sandwiched between large colorful ads for everything from gay bars to lingerie shops and day spas. David still drops me notes or sends me an email every now and then.

It doesn't take a genius to figure out why he's calling. The Amber Alert, stories in the news. He's obviously connected the dots and, knowing me, is sniffing around for the inside story.

"Hello, David."

"How are you holding up, old man?"

"Not so well."

"Really, really sorry to hear about your granddaughter."

"Thank you."

"She sounds like a good kid."

"More than you could ever write."

"Of course. Any new developments?"

Do I really want to bring another person into the picture at this point? "Sorry, David. I don't know anything more than what the police and the FBI may be telling you. Wish I did."

David hesitates on the other end of the line. "That doesn't sound like the Jerry Strickland I know."

I smile and say nothing.

"How about talking off the record then? Background only. You have my word."

One thing about David: he has always been en even-handed, straight shooter. His selective offering of investigation details in his stories even helped us smoke out a suspect or two.

"All right. But I don't have much time here."

"No problem. Do you know if the FBI suspects Marnee has been murdered?"

"To my knowledge, there's been no evidence found to that effect."

"I heard the father, Alex Butler, has been ruled out as a suspect. Is it true?"

"Maybe that's what they're telling the press."

"I gather you're not so sure."

"No."

"You said you don't have much time. Has there been any sort of contact with whoever took Marnee? Do they know where she is?"

Lucky guess. He's probably gotten this information already from another source and is just trying to confirm it with me.

"You know I can't comment on something like that, even if there has."

"Okay."

He's taking my answer as a yes.

"What about you, Jerry? This is the third time I've tried reaching you. I'm sure you haven't just been waiting around by the phone."

It's my turn to hesitate. "Lets just say I've been looking into a few things. Nothing definite yet."

"What kind of things?"

A few years after Rebecca went to prison, Wilhelm also wrote a short series of follow-up pieces on Jacob Gramm. Gramm was suspected in at least two other killings, both in Pennsylvania. The investigation went on even after Gramm's death. Edgar had been assigned a new partner by then, a rookie detective named Michelle Quinn. I kept tabs, but only from afar. I never heard much from Edgar about it again, especially after he retired. I stopped saving any newspaper clippings about Rebecca or Gramm after

Rebecca's death because there didn't seem any point. Except for my own out-of-date files, it occurs to me Wilhelm may be more up to speed than anyone about Jacob Gramm and the Jackie Brenlou case.

"You remember the articles you wrote all those years ago about Rebecca and the shooting of Jacob Gramm and the follow up pieces you wrote years later?"

"Absolutely."

"You talked to a lot of other people besides Richmond PD, didn't you—FBI, Virginia State Police, local Pennsylvania detectives, Pennsylvania State Police?"

"Sure did."

"Do you keep a record or copies of all the stuff you've ever written?"

"Wonders of modern technology. Got every word archived on disk."

"I wonder if I could ask you to do me a favor."

"Anything."

"Go back and see if you can find any mention or anything at all related to someone named Mary Harper or a Lassiter Harper."

"Last name Harper? It doesn't ring a bell. But I'll look."

"Thanks, David."

"Are you telling me you think there might be some link between what's happened to your granddaughter and Jacob Gramm?"

"I'm just asking you to look, David, that's all."

"Okay. How do I reach you?"

I give him the new cell phone number.

"Got it," he says. "Look up stuff and call you about Jacob Gramm. Which reminds me, you do remember the new arrest that happened last year?"

"New arrest. What new arrest?"

"In Pennsylvania. I sent you an email with a link to an article about it."

"Email?" This was news to me. "I never saw it. I hardly ever check email."

"Maybe it got lost in your junk mail. Anyway, I just came across it in some of my old email files again the other day. I'm pulling up something right now. Here we go. It was in Chester, the site of Gramm's second murder, where he killed the African- American girl. They arrested a sixty- year- old schoolteacher last year. Who'd have figured after all this time? But they got a DNA match. Turns out the teacher was Gramm's accomplice, at least in that killing."

"Gramm had an accomplice?"

"Yeah. I thought you knew."

"You remember any of the details?"

"Not really. I can look up the article again if you'd like. I think there was drinking involved. Gramm was a homicidal maniac, that was for sure."

No one needed to tell me. I stare at the kitchen table for a moment thinking.

"You still there, Jerry?"

"Yeah. Thanks, David. I gotta go."

"All right. You still want me to check out those other articles?"

"That would be great. Call me later if you find anything."

"Will do."

The line goes silent. What began as a weak connection to some boot prints seems as though it could be blossoming into something altogether different. I feel a tremor in my soul. My hand shudders as I hang up the phone.

Twenty-Nine

"Dad?" Lori answers on the first ring.

"Lori, you okay?"

"Fine. I was trying to call you but the line was busy."

"Is anything happening out there?"

"Yes. But a big blue BMW pulled into the driveway at the house about ten minutes ago."

"All right. You see anybody?"

"An older man. Thin and balding, wearing a sport coat. He went inside the house."

"Was he alone?"

"I didn't see anyone else."

"Okay. You don't move. Just stay in your car and keep an eye out. No matter what happens, don't do anything until we get there, do you understand?"

"I understand." She hangs up the line.

Colin leans over me, looking concerned. "Was that Mom?"

"Yes." I push up the from the kitchen chair. "You got your car keys handy?"

"Sure, right here." He picks them up from where he lay them on the counter.

"Let's go."

"Where are we heading?"

"We need to drive back out to Glenn Allen."

"Okay."

"And we need to phone Hal Ford on the way and have him meet us out there, and I need to head into the bedroom to get my .38."

• • •

My .38 lay snug in its holster at my side that afternoon years before, the yellowed linoleum corridors of the old Medical College of Virginia hospital doing little to brighten my spirits as I crossed the glass-enclosed bridge to the newer, multi-story building where Rebecca lay dying. Rebecca was napping and I needed to roam, if only for a short while to grab a cup of coffee from one of the vending machines outside the cafeteria. How I ended up in the old building next door I'm not sure. My mind was fuzzy with grief and lack of sleep.

Stepping off the elevator on Rebecca's ward again, I was shocked to see her outside her room unsteadily making her way toward me trailing her IV pole. A nurse rushed from behind her desk to help, but I waved her off as I swept Rebecca into my arms, guiding her back the way she'd come.

"There you are."

"I thought you were asleep. I was just taking a walk. You shouldn't be out of your room."

Her face seemed infused with a different light, as if she were already catching glimpses of heaven.

"I need to tell you something important, Jerry."

I got her situated back in her room and pulled a chair up close to her bed. "Sure, darling. Anything." I took her hand in mine.

With her other, she reached out ran her fingers along the side of my face. "How are you feeling?"

"How am I feeling?"

"Yes."

"I'm okay. How about you?"

"I'm seeing lots of things in my mind. Things I didn't know were there before."

"Of course." She was on morphine for the pain. *I wasn't sure if it was she or the drug talking.*

"You're in danger, Jerry."

"Me?"

"Yes. And you may soon be in a lot more."

"I don't—"

"No, listen. I was praying just now as I was awaking. The sun was streaming through the edge of the curtains just there." She pointed toward the window where the late afternoon sun was still angling along the sill. *"And as I prayed, the Lord showed me a vision. He showed me things, Jerry. You have no idea. He told me what I have to do. He told me I have to keep you safe."*

"Keep me safe from what?"

"Oh, darling, don't you see? It's here right now. It's all around you."

I looked around at the quiet of her room, at all the equipment and glowing monitors, at the IV pole with bags of liquid medicine dripping into her veins. "I don't understand."

"Don't worry," she said. "You will."

• • •

By the time we arrive there is no BMW next to the Chevy in the driveway at Mary Harper's house.

Lori's car is parked down the street a ways. It leaves the curb as we come into view; she guns the accelerator, and sweeps up beside us. The sound of the little dog barking from inside the house greets us as soon as we step from our cars. Through the front picture window, you can see it jumping up and down on the couch where it can look out at us.

"You just missed him," Lori says. "He left here only a minute ago. I was hoping you might spot him on the way in."

"Lassiter? An older man?"

"Yes. That was him."

I look down the street. "Which way did he go?"

"The same way you just came from."

"We didn't see him. He must have cleared the neighborhood just before we entered. You see anything else?"

"No. The house blocked part of his car. I just caught sight of him climbing in and driving off. I wasn't sure what to do. I thought about trying to follow him, but then I thought Marnee might be here inside the house."

Hal Ford's cruiser turns the corner down the street. The Crown Vic's lights are flashing as he sails toward us before screeching to a halt next to our cars. He throws his door open and leaps out.

"All right, Jerry. What's the big panic about?"

"We just missed it. The BMW left here a couple of minutes ago."

"How do you know that?"

"Lori here was keeping watch down the street."

"What?" He turns to Lori. "Mrs. Butler, this is not a good idea—"

"Just hear me out, Hal. Let's clear this house, first, and meet the lady inside. Then we can talk."

The dog has kept up its incessant barking from inside. Ford turns to look at the house. "This is the woman's house you been checking out, right? Mary Harper? The mystery woman with the boots?"

"That's the one."

His gaze turns back to me. "Dog seems upset."

I nod, turning to stare through the glass at the pitiful beast, wishing I had brought another half-eaten taco. "Maybe it's just his M.O."

"Let's hope."

The four of us step up to the front stoop and ring the doorbell, which only causes the dog to howl and bark even louder. No one answers the door, so we try again. Still no answer.

"Maybe she fell asleep," Colin suggests.

"That quickly?" I try the front door, but it's locked tight.

"Well. She's old."

Ford peers through the picture window. "Let's have a look around back."

Out back, we pull open the screen and knock on the kitchen door. This, of course, causes the dog inside to become even more enraged, howling to beat the band. We try again, knocking louder. The frame of the door shakes, but still no response.

"It's only been five minutes since her brother left. Something must be wrong." I peer in through the window beside the door. Everything in the kitchen appears to be in order. A bowl and a coffee cup lie on the counter next to the stove, but otherwise the place looks neat as a pin.

"Did she seem hard of hearing when you talked to her before?"

Colin shakes his head. "Not that I could tell. She didn't seem to have any problem understanding me."

I reach down and try the handle of the door, which turns easily in my hand. "It's open."

Hal steps in beside me. "I hope you've got justification to give me probable cause here."

He pushes open the door and steps inside. We all follow. But instead of coming to confront us as I expect, the tiny dog, still barking, appears to retreat from its post in the living room to one of the side bedrooms.

All the lights are off. Sunshine streaming in through the windows provides the only illumination. A trace of cinnamon lingers on the air, perhaps from a morning's baking. The dog seems to be running around now, its paws making staccato thumping sounds through the wall.

Ford draws his Glock and releases the safety. "Anybody home?" he hollers.

Nothing.

We make our way into the living room. A pincushion sofa and recliner face a plain wooden coffee table. An old television stares out from within the confines of a maple entertainment center. Covered by glass doors, the fireplace is stained black and looks well used. Packing boxes line one wall.

Everything else appears to be in good order, books lined in organized fashion along shelves on either side of the mantle, pillows neatly arrayed across the couch. The dog yelps from the bedroom.

"Anybody home?"

Still no response.

"Looks like nobody's here."

"Mmmm," I mumble to myself. The dog is panting now, not too far away.

"You sure about this, Jerry?" Ford gives me a long look. "If the woman's not here—"

"That's her Chevy in the driveway."

He nods.

We step around the corner to look through the open bedroom door. The dog barks and I spot him again, staring at us with bright eyes, his tongue hanging out of his mouth at the foot of the bed.

The little thing obviously knows more than we do. Its paw prints are everywhere: on the carpet, the bedspread, and the overstuffed chair.

Paw prints the color of blood.

Thirty

After calling it in, we look over the scene. There is enough gore and upheaval in the bedroom of Mary Harper's house to confirm something horrific has taken place here. But no Mary Harper. A dressing chair covered in blood lies on its back on the floor. In addition to the dog's prints, the sheets and sham on the bed, though still made up, are covered with bloody handprints and the wrinkled signs of someone reaching out to grab hold of them. A large patch of blood stains the carpet around the fallen chair. The closet door hangs open, a lamp on the bed stand has crashed to the floor, and signs of a struggle are evident elsewhere, even heading out into the hall.

Henrico County Police will be here within minutes and the FBI won't be far behind.

"Someone put up a good fight." I bend over, leaning on my cane, to get a closer look at some silver fragments on the carpet. "That look like a piece of jewelry to you?"

Colin stoops down to see it. "Yeah. It's a broken necklace."

"Wow," Colin says from over my shoulder.

"Recognize it?"

He nods. "Mrs. Harper was wearing it when I talked to her earlier."

"This is probably her blood then, too," Ford says.

Lori has remained outside the doorway to the bedroom.

"You think he killed her while I was right down the street?" Her hand covers her mouth.

I don't get to answer before the rumble of a police cruiser and flashing lights on the bedroom wall announces HPD's arrival.

After a flurry of questions, the officers and Ford help secure the scene.

Colin and Lori and I retreat to the front stoop to await further questioning. Sweat pours off of my brow. Someone hands me a plastic bottle of water that tastes like warm bile, but I drink it anyway.

A few moments later, a black Chevy Suburban with federal plates guns down the street toward us, pulling to a fast stop at the curb. Agent Markinson hops out followed by a team of agents.

Ford joins us on the stoop and looks at Markinson.

"All right, Jerry. You want to try to explain to us what's going on here now?"

I take another swig of water before making eye contact with the FBI agent. "I'll tell you what's going on. We need to find out where Lassiter Harper was working and living the year Jackie Brentlou was murdered. We need to find out if he ever hung around with or came into contact with Jacob Gramm."

Thirty-One

*R*ebecca remained a faithful member of Gideon Baptist while
in prison. Other members of the church corresponded with
her regularly and sent things out to Goochland she needed.
After the first year, she told me to stop bringing anything. She
just wanted to see me, she said, and the church was supplying
all her physical needs.

Sometime after she passed, a couple of deacons from the
church stopped by my house after work one evening to visit me.
I can't recall their names: middle-aged black men with receding
hairlines, one with wire-rimmed glasses one without.

We sat in the den, I in a straight-backed chair pulled
from the dining room and the two visitors on the blue slipcover
couch Rebecca had saved up to buy and purchased just a few
weeks before she shot Jacob Gramm. I didn't have anything else
in the house, so I asked them if they wanted coffee.

"No thanks, Jerry," the spectacled man said. "We just
wanted to come by and see how you were doing."

I knew, of course, there was a certain spiritual and social
obligation to the question, but behind the man's words, I sensed
a genuine desire to have an answer. So I gave him one.

"I want no more part of a God that would take Rebecca
away the way he did."

"All right."

"To see her suffer at the end was the worst."

The second deacon cleared his throat as if he'd eaten something foul for lunch, but Mr. Wire-rim seemed unfazed by my response. He just nodded. "I know how you feel," *he said.* "My son died of a drug overdose seven years ago. Straight A student. He would have been a senior in college today."

I didn't know what to say to that.

"Don't be afraid to tell God how you feel, Jerry. He can take it. Read Job sometime, read the Psalms."

I said nothing.

"Is there anything we can do for you? Anything we can bring you?" *the second deacon asked.*

I shook my head. "Not really."

"How are you fixed for meals?"

"I'm getting by."

"The church has a special meals ministry. Works like a well-oiled machine. Volunteers drop off the food every evening, no questions asked. You don't even have to talk to them if you don't want."

I'd dropped a few pounds since Rebecca's passing, but the truth was I didn't feel much like eating. "I'll think about it, thanks for your concern."

"You're a sergeant with the RPD, I understand," *the first deacon said.*

"That's correct."

"Rebecca talked about you all the time at church and in small group fellowship. I hope you don't mind, I almost feel like I know you."

"It was Rebecca's way," *I said, although the intrusion irritated me.*

"None of us really knows the truth about what happened between Rebecca and that murderer fella, but God works in mysterious ways sometimes."

Mysterious indeed.

"I know the last few years can't have been easy for you. If there's ever anything we at the church can do for you, anything *at all, day or night, you just give us a call."*

"But I haven't set foot inside your building in years."

"Doesn't matter. Rebecca was your wife. We're always here for you. You're never alone."

"No offense, gentlemen. But I feel pretty alone right now. Whether you're here or not."

"We understand, Jerry. We understand."

Did they? Maybe a little, especially the deacon with the glasses.

If there is a family gospel it's this: one way or another, you pass on all your joys and passions, sins, hurts, and fears to those you love. I don't know if there is any way of getting around this simple truth.

Still, I kept a secret from those deacons that afternoon, one I've never shared with anyone.

At the graveside following Rebecca's funeral, I stood with Rebecca's parents and Lori in the sun. The bright afternoon had ushered in a late February warm spell. The temperature had climbed into the sixties. Rebecca's father spoke a few words before they lowered the casket into the ground. I fought back tears.

All at once, what I can only describe as a current of energy pulsed through me, a sun-backed shudder of light.

I suppose some neuroscientist could explain away the experience as a purely natural phenomenon, the brain's physiological reaction to extreme emotion. But as long as I live I will never forget that sensation.

It felt like wings.

•   •   •

Lassiter spends over an hour digging his sister's grave. As deep he can make it. He covers her body with two or three feet of earth, leaves, and ferns, and rolls a couple of decent sized stones over top, dressing up the ground cover to make it look as natural as possible.

He's crossed a line. Extracting the little girl's toe was a

simple surgical procedure, and he did a proper job of it. But this is different. He's killed again, and it wasn't as hard as he thought. In Mary's case, he can almost convince himself it was the right and merciful thing to do.

He wipes away a tear as the woods recede in his rearview mirror.

No getting around it anymore, his worst-case scenario is upon him. He can't believe it's come down to this. He's not some kind of monster. Not like Gramm. He's lived a good life. Gone to mass every now and then with Carol, given money to good causes, and, except for the little problem with Atlantic City, mostly kept his nose clean.

He thinks about the little town in Mexico again, memories of the woman's soft body and how it all might work, if he can eliminate the only people who might connect him to the killings. He's got a few good years left in him. Even if someone does make a connection, they may never find him, at least until he's so old or demented he won't care anymore. Like Mary.

It'll be hard on Carol, of course. After he scuttles the boat, she'll imagine the worst, and there will be a search for his body. The guys from Atlantic City may even come calling, but he can't see them squeezing a defenseless widow. Either way, he'll find some way to get money to her.

His mind turns back to the task at hand. He wonders how the little girl managed to get hold of what she did, how the girl's father connected it to his sister.

Who would have thought Mary would have used one of his receipts from the motor inn all those years ago in her note to the cop? No one had ever able to connect the dots before.

It's like a lot of things, he supposes: subject to inertia, the lost details of time, the overlooked pieces to puzzles that may never be solved. Except now someone threatens to pull in a right piece.

He needs to remain calm. He's still got enough of the Scopolamine he was able to steal from the old Walter Reed warehouse. For anyone else who has to die, from the bratty kid to her meddling lawyer of a father, he'll try to make sure they do so peacefully.

Lassiter is no monster. They won't feel a thing.

• • •

Back at Lori's house, the heat hasn't kept a few curious neighbors and other gawkers from sitting in their lawn chairs behind police tape outside. They've erected a makeshift flower display in honor of Marnee as if she is already dead.

Inside, the dining room buzzes with activity. With only a short while left until the ransom exchange, Agent Caldwell and an assortment of FBI personnel assigned to her task force are hunched over laptop computers and working the phones.

I stand to one side and try to stay out of everybody's way. Lori, in a corner by the entrance to the living room, is talking to someone on her cell.

At least now we have a suspect.

It didn't take Hal Ford and Agent Markinson long to see the logic in what I told them, and even less time to confirm Lassiter Harper had indeed lived just South of Richmond at the time of Jackie Brentlou's murder, while working in Petersburg at Ft. Lee. Forensics is running more tests to see if Mary Harper's boots left the prints found at the scene of Marnee's abduction. The prints are identical, just as I surmised, and apparently in his haste Lassiter wasn't able to scrub off every microscopic bit of soil residue. All law enforcement agencies have been issued a Be-On-The-Lookout for Lassiter Harper, age sixty-eight, along with the plate number and description of his car.

The ransom exchange is still on, but everyone worries about the state of the kidnapper's mind. Harper doesn't know we found the blood at his sister's house in Glen Allen, doesn't know we're on to his past connection with Jacob Gramm.

Lori finishes her phone call, comes over and gives me a hug. She's washed up a little and put on some makeup, changed into a cotton dress with sandals, but it can't mask her being sick with fear.

"I'm sorry for doubting for you, Dad."

"Forget it. Are you all right?"

"Praying the ransom is going to work."

"Me, too. Where's Alex?"

"He's out back in the trailer talking with the FBI. They're prepping him for dropping off the money."

I follow her into the kitchen. Colin is there, too. Lori sits me down in a chair and rinses off a washcloth at the sink, turning to dab it against the wound above my hairline. "I heard you took a nasty fall back at the house."

"It was nothing." I take a deep breath and look around the kitchen for a moment at the stainless steel appliances, the oversized copper-bottomed pots and pans hanging from a rack over a center island. The refrigerator hums. Water ticks in a recently boiled kettle on the stove. I remember sitting here eating Cornflakes with Marnee one weekend morning when I was visiting not long ago. Marnee loves Cornflakes. Loves them with cold milk and sliced strawberries.

An electronic chirp pierces the air.

"My phone." Lori picks it up from where she's placed it on the table. "Hello." She stands up and turns away from the table listening to her whomever is speaking, holding her index finger in her opposite ear so she can hear clearly. Still listening, she steps out the door heading back toward the dining room.

Colin picks up an empty glass from the table. "You want some water?" His face seems to have taken on a darker pallor since seeing all the blood at Mary Harper's house.

Maybe it's driven home what could happen, what might be happening right now to Marnee.

"No thanks. I'm okay."

"It's stinking hot out there today."

He reaches down to adjust one of the flip-flips covering the bottoms of his tanned feet. A ceiling fan pushes the air over our heads. I glance at the clock on the wall. Less than two hours to go until the exchange.

Heavy footfalls signal a flurry of activity from the other room.

Lori bursts back into the kitchen.

"What's wrong?" I start to stand.

"It's Alex."

"Alex? I thought you said he was out back in the trailer with the FBI."

"He was. But he's gone."

"Gone? Where?"

"No one knows."

Thirty-Two

"Unmarked bills."

"What?" Agent Barbara Caldwell looks at me with concern.

"That looks like what's happening here."

The mobile FBI command post is housed in a nondescript thirty foot RV emblazoned with the bureau's crest. Lori, Colin, and I stand with Agents Caldwell and Markinson next to the trailer doorway.

"Harper's smart," I continue. "He knows you people will be all over him if he does a normal ransom exchange. He contacted Alex. Remember, he's talked with Alex before."

"So he figures why not deal direct," Caldwell says. "Go after untraceable money."

"It's a safe bet." I look at Colin. "Didn't your dad mention something about offshore accounts?"

"Yeah," Colin says. "Something like that."

"Stupid," Markinson says. "If Alex thinks it'll give him a better shot at getting Marnee back safely, he's in for a rude awakening. That's not how the game is played."

He looks at Agent Caldwell. "What happened out here?"

"The tech was just starting to get him set up for a trial run of the wire he was supposed to wear," she says. "Tech forgot some gear in the dining room and went back in the house to retrieve it. Says he left Mr. Butler alone for less than a minute, but when he got back out to the trailer Mr. Butler was gone."

I lean on the side of the RV. "How do you know for sure he's trying to deal with the kidnapper by himself?"

Caldwell holds up a plain piece of computer printer paper with a note written in felt tip black ink.

SORRY NEED TO GO THIS ALONE.

"That look like your husband's writing, Ms. Butler?"

Lori bites her lip and nods.

Markinson looks like a man facing the prospect of an operation suddenly gun awry. His operation. He asks me:

"Any chance your son-in-law has been in on this thing from the beginning?"

Lori raises both hands to her head as if to fend off the possibility.

"No way," Colin interrupts. No, no way."

I put a hand on Colin's shoulder. "We can't say anything for sure. There's always the possibility Harper has threatened to kill Marnee if Alex doesn't cooperate. We've already seen how far he was willing to go with his sister."

"All right, Jerry, you're making some sense," Markinson says. He turns away from me and looks at across at Caldwell. "We need to get the team together to discuss the possibilities and figure out what's happening. Looks like we have a double manhunt on our hands."

I don't like the idea of being turfed again, but there it is. Whatever Alex is up to, whether innocent or not, it can't be making things any better for Marnee.

Caldwell and Markinson leave us. Lori, Colin, and I head back into the house. As we're walking through the doorway into the kitchen, I look out the window toward the driveway at the line of unmarked federal cars and see a pair of agents in the front seat of one of the cars, a brown Dodge, facing the street.

But I also recognize the back of a woman's head in the rear seat, a shape I could never forget.

Lori can't seem to sit still. She heads toward the entryway leading to the front of the house. "I'll be right back, Dad. I want to talk to a couple of the other agents in the dining room. See if either of them knows anything more." She disappears through the door.

I glance out the window again, wondering if I'm seeing things. The car with the woman in it has started up and begun to pull out of the driveway. The woman turns her head to look at me for an instant.

There's no doubt: it's Rebecca. Except it can't be. I must be suffering from a concussion or some kind of end-of-life delusion.

The Dodge continues down the driveway.

"Colin." Before he can pull his chair out all the way, I grab him by the arm. "Get your car keys out again."

"Why?"

I point out the window. "We need to follow that car heading out the driveway."

He turns to see where I am pointing. "That looks like one of those FBI cars. Why do we need to follow them?"

"Just do it. I'll explain on the way."

"What about Mom?"

"No time. Let's go."

Thirty-Three

"This is crazy, Granddad."

"Maybe. Calm down."

The Dodge has gained a two-block lead on us, but we've been able to keep it in sight.

"Why do you want to follow these people? I mean, first Dad takes off and now we're taking off too?"

"Just focus on your driving right now. I haven't steered you wrong yet, have I? We need to keep up with that car."

"Okay. Okay."

The Dodge seems to be proceeding at a regular rate of speed. After a light it moves into a lane leading to an on ramp for the Chippenham Parkway.

"Where are they going?"

"I don't know. But we don't want to lose them."

Colin floors it and just misses getting caught at the light, but another car pulls right in front of us, slowing us down. Seconds later, we accelerate up the ramp onto the expressway. We can barely make out the Dodge following behind a tractor-trailer about a quarter mile in the distance.

"Step on it."

Colin hits the gas, and it doesn't take long before we're following along behind the Dodge again at a comfortable distance.

"Okay," he says. "You aren't going to tell me any more?"

"Look." I pause for a second or two. "You remember down in the basement where you saw all those photos?"

"Yeah."

"Your grandmother used to work with sometimes down there."

"She did?"

"This may sound crazy, but I feel like she is telling me to follow that car." I figure I better leave out the fact I'm actually seeing her.

"Grandma's telling you?" He glances across at me.

"That's right."

"Grandma who's been dead for what, fifteen years?"

"Yes. Keep an eye on that car."

"I am. I am. But I'm also wondering if I should be taking you to a hospital."

"You've been with me all day. You see me doing anything delusional?"

"Up until now, no."

"Then you just have to trust me on this one."

The Dodge slows up ahead.

Rebecca hasn't turned her head to look back at me again, but I can still make out her profile clearly. I'm afraid to ask Colin if he sees her sitting in the back of the Dodge, too.

"Easy," I say. "We don't want to get too close and spook them."

"I'm the one who's spooked." Colin lets off the accelerator. "Looks like they're taking the next exit."

"Midlothian Turnpike. Not good." The turnpike is a miles-long straightaway lined with shopping centers and dotted by traffic signals, and at this hour, it's filled with bumper-to-bumper traffic. "You'll need to get a little closer or we'll lose them."

Colin speeds up, but as we pull off the highway a tollbooth looms.

"You want me to run it?"

"No, we can't risk getting pulled over."

Fortunately, the line moves quickly. Colin is able to dig out a couple of quarters and toss them into the toll basket, but by the time we turn onto Midlothian, the Dodge is nowhere in sight.

"We lost them," Colin says.

"Keep driving this direction. Check all the gas stations, office buildings, and shopping centers on your side. I'll watch the ones on this side. They must have turned in somewhere."

"All right."

Traffic on the turnpike is heavy as usual. We cruise on through a few more lights. Just beyond the parking lot of a large hotel on my side, I spy a row of single story commercial buildings with a parallel access road buffering the structures from the turnpike. No sign of Rebecca or the Dodge. I'm about to give up hope when I spot the car parked along the access road in front of a professional office.

"There."

Colin sees it, too. We stop on the access road about a hundred and fifty yards short of the Dodge. The sun is dipping lower in the sky, reflecting off the glass of a multi-story bank next-door.

I squint into the light.

Up ahead, I see Rebecca push open her car door and exit the Dodge. She starts walking toward the professional building.

"What do you see?" I ask Colin.

He cups a hand over his eyes to shield them from the glare. "I see the car, but it's empty."

"Nothing else?"

"Nope."

I was afraid he'd say that.

I make a motion toward the Dodge. "Let's get up there and check out the building."

"Whatever you say."

Rebecca disappears somewhere around the front of the structure. Colin floors it again and we speed to a hard stop behind the brown sedan, which up close does indeed look empty. I turn to look at the building.

"Wait a minute," Colin says. "I recognize this place. It's my dad's office."

I've never seen it before. "What are you talking about? His office is downtown."

"No. This is a smaller one his firm uses, like a satellite or something. He brought me out here once a couple of years ago."

Thirty-Four

The satellite offices of Butler, Allen & Davis, Attorneys at Law command a marquis location at the front of a fashionable office park. It's well after five o'clock and the parking lot looks deserted.

"Time to move." I pull open the glove box and lift out the .38.

"Maybe I should take the gun," Colin says.

He's had training. I'm the one who gave it to him when he turned fourteen. I taught Lori how to handle a firearm when she was growing up, too.

"Sorry, bud. Not this go-round."

The gun is in a hip holster. I attach it to the belt holding up my khaki pants. It's hot enough outside, I leave my shirt tucked out, pulling it over top of the holster to hide I'm carrying. Something tells me there's not much of a hurry.

The Dodge's doors are locked.

"What now?"

"Let's check out the building."

The front door of the office is locked too, so we head around back. One side of the building faces a neatly mulched planting bed and more empty parking spaces. Across the pavement a chain link fence is intertwined with vines and blocks the view of whatever is next door. No sign of Rebecca, or anyone else for that matter.

A storage shed sits at the back of the lot, behind which hovers a stand of oversized bushes. As we edge closer, I catch sight of something: the dark edge of a bumper poking out from beneath the hedge.

"You see what I see?"

"What?"

"I'm not sure. Back there behind the storage shed."

The closer we get, the more a form begins to take shape among the branches. Someone has attempted to conceal it with stalks of bamboo, a stand of which is growing along the back fence.

"Looks like someone's hidden a car back here."

Colin jogs on ahead.

"Take it easy now." I scan the area and glance back at the building for a moment. I wonder if Rebecca has managed to walk through a wall or something, or if she is sill somewhere outside, watching us. I wonder if I am still in complete possession of my sanity.

Colin has already started to pull the bamboo off the windshield behind the shed. There's no disguising Lassiter Harper's dark blue BMW with the D.C. plates. I move in beside it.

"Is it locked?" Colin asks.

I try the door and it opens. Interesting. The car is empty. I find the control button and pop the trunk, but it, too, contains nothing.

"What do we do now?" Colin stops pulling off the strands of bamboo.

"Don't touch anything more. This car will have to be gone over by forensics."

"All right."

"Let's check around the other side of the building."

By the back door a long brown dumpster perches on the pavement. It's blocked from the rear entrance by a privacy screen. Behind the screen a round metal table and three folding chairs occupy a smoking area with a fireproof cigarette receptacle. The back door itself is heavy metal construction with a round, brushed metal doorknob and dead bolt.

Colin tries the knob, but it's a waste of time. I examine the entrance to see if there's any other way of breaking in, but it doesn't look promising, not without a heavy crowbar or serious lock-picking tools.

I look toward the back corner of the building. "Maybe there's another door."

Colin starts around the opposite side of the structure.

"Hold up. Let's take it slow."

Crouching, we peek around the corner. Sure enough, a small atrium pushes out from the long wall along the side of the building with a glass door framing windows, planting beds, and more parking spaces.

"Righteous," Colin whispers. "Guess we'll check out this other entrance."

But looking down along the parking lot, I stop him. "Hold on a sec." I grab hold of his arm and point with my other hand.

The parking lot at this side of the building connects to a tree lined lot from another building next door. Parked in the shadows under one of the far maples sits Alex's Escalade.

Thirty-Five

"**D**ad's here?"

"Looks that way."

"What's going on?"

"Good question. Maybe he's trying to get the unmarked money together."

I survey the scene. The lot, the vehicle, and the entrance remain quiet.

"What do we do now?"

"We hope that other door's open or find a different way inside." I check the feel of my gun against my belt.

"Shouldn't we call someone?"

"Not yet."

"But weren't those FBI agents driving the car out front?"

"Somehow I don't think so."

"What do you mean?'

"What I mean is there's a lot more going on here than meets the eye."

"Yeah. Okay."

I break from cover, Colin follows, and we make toward the atrium. This entrance to the law practice is almost as impressive as the rest of the building. A white, pillared portico frames the red brick wall offset on either side by a pair of twelve-foot high windows with black jalousied casements. Old Dominion money, I think, or at least Old Dominion tradition.

I remember back when Lori and Alex were first married. Alex had just graduated from law school before scoring a job with one of the city's largest law firms. He and Lori didn't have so much as a nickel to rub together between the two of them then, but they were in love. Sometimes they even reminded me of Rebecca and myself.

The office inside looks dark, but the door is unlocked. Is someone purposefully making this too easy? I pull the glass door open and we step into the entryway. A rush of cool air washes over us as the outside door thuds to a close behind us.

We stop and listen. An empty receptionist station stands before us. Big plants in one corner. The scent of freshly-shampooed carpet. Cleaning crew must have already finished working here for the day. Through an open door, a long hallway is visible and several side doors to other rooms. A water cooler motor purrs from the corner of the reception area. Other than that, silence.

I start for the doorway, signaling Colin to come along. Then a faint bump sounds from somewhere down the hall, like the sound a chair makes when it scrapes against a wall, followed by a muffled voice speaking.

I stop to listen, but before I can pull Colin back, he steps out into the corridor. More sounds of movement, then I catch sight of Alex's head peeking out from one of the far doorways. "Who's there? Oh, man. Colin, is that you?"

"Yeah." Colin glances back at me.

"How'd you get here?"

"Um. Drove."

"How'd you know I'd be here?"

"Uh." Colin looks back at me again.

I move out into the corridor beside him. "Because he came with me."

"Great." Alex says something else under his breath as he steps out from whatever room he's been in, closing the door behind him. His face is drawn, peaked even. "What are you two doing here?"

I try to look past him down the hallway. "You took off from the house and left a note. A lot of people are looking for you."

"Yeah, well..."

Why did I see Rebecca walking into this building? Is Marnee here, too? What kind of play is Alex making?

"Five-hundred thousand. You keep that kind of money around the office here, do you, Alex?"

Alex says nothing.

"Get our your cell phone," I tell Colin softly.

Alex's face seems to lose all its color. "Jerry, with all due respect, you don't know what you're talking about."

We stare at one another across the narrow hallway. He is wearing a brown T-shirt and blue jeans, out of uniform for the office.

He folds his arms across his chest. As a defense against what? I wonder. Surely, not his aged, wreck of a father-in-law and his teenaged son, who, truth be told, would like nothing better than to worship the ground Alex walks on if Alex would just quit screwing up things by acting like he's never grown beyond a teen himself.

"Make the call," I whisper to Colin.

He starts to dial the numbers on his phone as I reach for my .38.

"Hold it right there." Another voice.

From behind the door, Lassiter Harper emerges, pressing the snout of a sound suppressor barrel of a .40 caliber Glock against the side of Alex's head.

Thirty-Six

*E*dgar was behind the wheel that afternoon when our car bag phone began to ring. We had been waiting around most of the day for a court case that only ended in delay and were on our way back to the office to file our reports. As soon as we finished downtown, we planned to make another trip out to Jackie Brentlou's school where we planned to look through the files and gather more evidence in the hopes of linking something to Gramm.

"Jerry?" It was Rebecca on the line.

"Yeah, honey. How are you?"

"Where are you right now?"

"In the car with Ed." I gave her our location. "Why?"

"I need you to come and get me." She sounded scared and out of breath. Not like herself at all.

"What's wrong? Where are you?"

I glanced over at Ed who kept his eyes locked on the road. I could hear the shaking in Rebecca's voice.

She gave me an address. I took out my pen and began to write down the number and the street when it hit me.

"Wait a minute. That's Jacob Gramm's address."

I looked back across at Edgar, who was throwing me curious glances now, showed him the address, and made a circular motion with my hand to tell him to step on it.

Rebecca knew all about Gramm by this point, of course.

We'd talked about it every evening and she said she'd been praying about the Brentlou case day and night.

"Hurry," she said.

"What's happening there, Rebecca?" There was silence on the line.

"Rebecca?" I thought the car phone might have dropped the call.

"I'm in his apartment."

"Gramm's?"

"Yes."

"But how did you—?"

"I took the bus."

"Is Gramm there?"

"Yes."

"You need to get out of there."

"Don't worry. I'm okay. Gramm's no longer a problem."

"What do you mean no longer a problem?"

"He was going to kill her, Jerry. I saw what he was planning. Don't ask me how. I saw it. He was planning to grab her this afternoon."

"Who?"

"He's been watching her and today he was going to take her and kill her. There wasn't time. I couldn't reach you. I couldn't tell anyone else, and I knew you were downtown in court. It's not that far. I could get here on the bus in ten minutes. And then I did something terrible."

Ed gunned the engine as we passed through an intersection. My mind was reeling.

"What are you trying to tell me?"

"Don't you see? I stopped him."

"Stopped him how?"

"I had to do it. I tried confronting him, but it wasn't working."

"How'd you stop him, Rebecca?"

"I killed him, Jerry." Her tearful voice shook through the line. "I shot him with your gun."

• • •

"Looks as though we have a problem here." I glance at Colin, whose eyes, focused on the Glock, have grown as big as moons. His hand is frozen on the phone.

"Put the phone down, son." Harper shifts his stance so he can angle the gun at us as well. Colin sets the phone on the floor. "And Detective Strickland. I believe we've met before. Except I didn't know who you were then. Now I do. You can take that hand away from your revolver. Pretty clever trick, by the way, with the car."

My heart pounds, blood and life coursing through me as I haven't felt it for weeks, months, maybe even years. The heightened awareness precipitated by approaching death? It floods light-like through me now, absorbing every detail of the scene, every movement, every molecule. What do I have to fear from this man's gun? A quicker end to my inevitable demise?

But Harper seems to read my thoughts.

"It's not you, it's your son-in-law and your grandson I'm going to shoot, Detective. And then you. I need you to stand down." The kidnapper's forehead glistens with sweat.

"Where's Marnee?"

"You know, you and I are a lot alike, Detective. Great generation people. Not like these sniveling little baby boomers and generation whatevers. You and I understand how to get things done."

"You were with Jacob Gramm when he murdered Jackie Brentlou."

Harper smiles. "Very good, Detective. You're one smart man, but by the time anybody else begins to piece this all together, I'll be so far gone into my international retirement it won't matter."

"I've got news for you. People have already started to piece it together."

He seems to hesitate for the first time. I watch the gun for any sign of weakness.

But Harper recovers. "Your wife killed Gramm. Good riddance—he got what he deserved. The man was a lunatic. I never meant for that girl to die back then. Just so you know."

"I'm sure you didn't. Maybe we can work something out with the prosecutor."

"Don't try to play me, Detective. Neither of us was born yesterday."

"Fine." I look at Alex. "What's your role in all this?"

But Harper interrupts. "Don't you get it? Alex is my unwitting sugar daddy, not to mention brilliant cover story."

"He's getting you unmarked bills."

"Very good. Willing to play the hero to get his daughter back. Just like you, Detective. A bunch of great big heroes, we got here. I can almost admire that. But enough with the questions."

Alex starts to speak. "Jerry, he's—"

"Shut up." Harper points the gun between Alex's eyes, which stops him cold. "Detective, I want you to unfasten the holster holding that little pea shooter of yours and place it down nice and easy next to your grandson's phone."

I think it over for a moment. Giving my gun away goes against all of my training and what I have always taught. In any split-second confrontation, the major advantage goes to whoever moves first. In the old days, I would have raised my gun and put a bullet in Harper before the man had time to react.

But it isn't the old days anymore. I'm seeing visions of my dead wife, and I haven't been to the shooting range in years. I do as he instructs.

"Excellent. Now I want you two to put your hands in the air and mosey on down here and join us. No funny stuff."

Colin and I move slowly together down the hall. When we're almost abreast of them, Harper grabs Alex by the shoulder and yanks him back into the room he's just exited, motioning for us to follow.

It's a small conference room with a heavy wooden table and stylish office chairs on wheels.

"All right. This is going to look exactly how I want it to look." He and I stare at one another.

"You're the one holding the gun," I say. "Are you just making this part up as you go along?"

"It's true. I don't know exactly why Alex would have taken his own daughter hostage and asked for the ransom, but I think it may have something to do with one of those shady clients he's always defending. I think maybe he owes somebody a lot of money. Don't worry, I'll come up with some way to make it look convincing enough."

"Where's Marnee?" I ask again.

"Seminole Hill back of a vacant knit store—" The words tumble from Alex's mouth.

Harper shoots him in the leg.

Even with the suppressor, the bang from the shot is startling in such close quarters. Our ears take a couple of seconds to recover as Alex crumples to the floor. Blood speckles the chairs, the table, and the expensive blue carpet of the conference room.

The only good news, if my memory serves, Seminole Hill Shopping Center is only a short ways down the turnpike. Marnee—assuming she's still alive—may not be far away.

Alex moans as Harper bends over him. "What part of shut up did I not make clear to you?"

"Dad!" Colin kneels on the floor beside his wounded father.

Harper looks at me. "If I don't get the cooperation I want, the next bullet goes in the boy's head."

We glare at one another. Alex grits his teeth and moans some more, looking up at me with pleading eyes.

"So here's the way it's gotta go," Harper says. "First and foremost, we need everyone to empty their pockets. Especially you, Detective. Got a mobile phone? Have we joined the twenty-first century yet?"

"I left it in the car," I say, which is untrue.

"Pardon me if I don't believe you. Keep your hands in the air." He gestures with the gun, looking back at Alex and Colin for a moment as he does.

It's not a big opening, but it's the only one I'm going to get.

I lean against one of the chairs, shoving it straight at Harper. He takes a moment to recover before firing at me, missing, but gets off a second shot the moment I'm on him.

We hit the floor hard. Something burns in my arm. I grab him around the legs, but he manages to kick me away. Colin tries to help, but he's too late. Harper shoves me to the floor and points the gun at Colin's head.

"Don't want to fire off any more bullets, but I will if I have to."

I believe him.

I lay on the floor. My right arm is useless. It feels like it's about to explode.

"Then again, that wasn't too smart, Detective." Harper twists the gun around and points it at Colin's face.

"Don't." My eyes meet his. "You may need him to drag my body."

He holds for a moment, looking at me. Then he nods. "Just delaying the inevitable. No more tricks."

He makes quick work of frisking me, finds my cell phone and pockets it.

I glance at Colin and Alex across the floor.

"Here's how we're gonna leave this," Harper says. "Mr. Butler here is coming with me." He grabs Alex by the shirt and starts dragging him through the doorway and maneuvering him into the hall. "While you two fine gentlemen get to stay here."

"That's it?" I expected something more.

"Don't worry, Detective. You and the young man will be taken care of soon enough."

I have no idea what he's talking about, but I don't like the sounds of it. He slams the heavy wooden office door closed behind him. A click crosses the room as it's locked tight.

A few seconds later, we hear a scrapping sound along the carpet outside and the door shudders. Apparently, Harper has shoved some kind of heavy piece of furniture against it.

"What did he mean we'd be taken care of?" Colin looks nervous.

"I have no idea."

"You're bleeding pretty bad." He stumbles over his words, tears forming in the corners of his eyes. "And Dad was, too."

"I need you to calm down, Colin. Take deep breaths. You've had first aid training. You know how to make a tourniquet?"

He nods, breathing slowly, and seems to gather himself.

"Great. Tear off my shirt sleeve. Rip it into strips and tie it off above the wound."

He does just as I say. I grit my teeth and shake my head to try to keep from going into shock as he pulls the cloth taut. But the bleeding seems to slow.

Colin asks, "Are we going to die?"

"Not if we can help it."

"Dad was telling the truth, wasn't he? I mean about not working with the guy."

"It looks that way, but it doesn't do us much good right now."

"Why does this old dude want to kill us?"

"Finishing what he started by taking Marnee. He's deluded himself into thinking he can still get away with everything, and the truth is, if your little sister hadn't pulled that check and note out of the file in my basement and you and I hadn't been so persistent about those boot prints, he would have probably been right. Either way, he's all in now."

"But—"

"Shhhh." I put my finger to my lips. "Listen."

The whoosh of the building's central air slips through vents overhead and rinses down over us, the compressor humming somewhere through the exterior walls. Then the faint catch of the Escalade's engine cuts through the air. But instead of growing fainter, the noise grows louder until it sounds like it's right outside the building.

"Not good." I grab the table and push back up to my feet with Colin's help. "We need to figure out how to get out of here." I scan the room. "Now."

"Why? What's going on?"

"Harper's taking the BMW and leaving the Escalade here running. It's right outside this room."

"How come?"

"The building has zoned air-conditioning. He's hooked up a hose to the tailpipe and is pumping the exhaust in through the ventilation system." As if to confirm my fears, a faint ribbon of white smoke seeps through the vent overhead.

"Doesn't that mean carbon monoxide or something?"

"Uh-huh. The catalytic converter burns up most of it, but there'll be enough to kill us soon enough."

"What's that smoke?"

"What you see coming though the vent is just the coolant in the system being vaporized. It'll go away. But it's going to get awfully uncomfortable trying to breathe in here in a few minutes, not like in the old movies where people used their car exhausts to commit painless suicide."

"This isn't happening." Colin runs his fingers through his hair.

I check out the ceiling and walls. Solid brick and drywall construction, not much chance for escape there. Which leaves us with the door.

Colin sees the same thing and, sensing the urgency, rears up and kicks for all he's worth at the heavy wooden door with the bottom of one of his feet. It barely vibrates. Not a good sign. He tries a second time with the same result.

"We're going to die here, Granddad. We're going to just choke to death."

The smell of unburned gasoline from the car's emissions permeates the room. Colin kicks at the door again to no effect. I grab him by the shirt. "We need to try to hit it together."

"All right."

I lie down flat on my back, slide myself up to the base of the door and pull my knees up to my chest. "I'll kick it with my heels from the bottom and you kick higher up."

"Got it."

"On three."

We strike the door hard.

It seems to shake a little more, but it's still a long way from giving in.

"Again."

Not much different.

"Again."

The same.

We hit the door several more times. Maybe it's making some difference, maybe not. Colin keeps on kicking, but I need to stop for a minute, out of breath.

The room is growing cloudy with smoke. I close my eyes to see images of Rebecca and her father's church, and maybe the light to come. Then I'm swept back to the tunnels of my youth, a cave on our old farm where a couple of my buddies and I used to squirm into a hillside, mindful of stinging ants and snakes. I mutter a feeble prayer.

The wall seems to shift of its own accord, and for a few seconds, I don't know how, it seems as if I can see right through. On the opposite side stands Rebecca, smiling. I look back at the door. Still shut tight.

"Can you help us?"

"What'd you say?" Colin doesn't see her.

"You need to go," Rebeccca says. She steps to the side, drawing her hand across the door, and it moves.

"What's happening?" Colin is still kicking.

"The door's moving. I think it's working. Hit it harder."

He kicks again, and again. Then he rears back and makes a leap at the wood, bringing the full weight of his body against it. The door gives way with a thunderous crack, crashing to the hallway floor.

"Yeaaaaah! Who's the man?" Colin has fallen through with the door into the hallway, but he jumps up thumping his chest. "Yeaahhhh!"

Thirty-Seven

*J*acob Gramm lay facedown in the middle of a throw rug on his hardwood floor. The rug had once been green in color, apparently, with some sort of pattern swirl. Now it was a disgusting maroon saturated with Gramm's blood. Some type of presence hung in the air, too, as if a kind of spiritual warfare had taken place.

"Holy mother." Edgar whistled under his breath.

We'd scrambled up the stairs and burst in through the door of the apartment, weapons drawn in cover formation, only to find a quiet room. A dog barked somewhere outside. Otherwise there appeared to be no activity in the building. Apparently, no neighbors had called in to report a shot fired.

"Jerry?" At the far end of the room facing an open window, Rebecca sat in a plain, straight back chair with her hands folded in her lap and her back to us.

I stepped around the body. A single shot. Straight through the face and up into the brain. That's all it took, from the looks of it. Rebecca couldn't have been more efficient if she'd been a contract killer.

"I'm here." I rushed to her side, placing a hand on her arm. I was still trying to wrap my mind around the entire scene.

Her shoulders began to heave. She nodded toward the open window. "I managed to get it open. I needed to get some air." I took a deep breath of the breeze rushing in.

She still held my old police special, also a .38, in her hand.

"Let me have the gun, Rebecca."

"All right."

Edgar and I had already donned latex gloves. She gave me the gun without protest, her tears beginning again. I knelt on one knee and bent into her, folding her into my arms, both of us rocking with the force of her sobs. Edgar went to look over the rest of the apartment, making himself scarce.

"Tell me again what happened," *I said. She had already tried to explain her motive to me on the phone.*

"Like I told you, he was about to kill her."

"Who?"

"A girl."

"What girl?"

"He'd been watching her. He was planning to wait for her in some woods she always walked by on her way home from school. He was going to do it this afternoon, right this very moment, in fact. Somebody had to stop him. He was planning to do terrible things to her."

I was trying to imagine how all this would sound to a jury, how Rebecca would be faced with the prospect of proving the validity of her story in front of a skeptical judge and prosecutor, not to mention a doubtful public. She'd be labeled a nut.

Edgar, of course, had little or no idea how or why Rebecca was here. What would he think if Rebecca tried to make such a defense? Whenever he'd asked me why I talked on the phone with Rebecca so often when we were working a case, I'd managed to deflect his questions, and he'd never pushed me any further.

We knew Gramm was one evil operator. We were sure he'd murdered Jackie Brentlou, for starters. We were well along the way to making a solid case.

But even if Rebecca were right about what Gramm had intended to do this afternoon, what we were looking at on the floor of this apartment was murder, plain and simple. Preemptive murder.

Even if we found some incriminating physical evidence, a photo or a journal entry or some other written plans about Graham's supposed intended target, there was little hope of corroborating Rebecca's story. How could she explain knowing for certain he was about to strike? How could she ever hope to prove what Gramm had been thinking?

The rumors would begin to fly either way. A detective's wife and a killer. She was found in his apartment and he was lying dead on the floor. She was involved with the man, some would say. Maybe I was the one who really offed the guy in a jealous rage and for whatever twisted reason Rebecca was taking the fall. We couldn't hide the truth, could we?

I should have known it could one day come down to this. Rebecca with her abilities, the two of us always pushing the edge in pursuit of...what? Evil? Or was it something closer to ourselves?

I should never have involved her with my work in the first place, or quit the job; I should have gotten both of us as far away as from police work as I could.

But it was too late for that now.

I looked down at the gun in my gloved hand.

"How do you want to handle this, boss?"

I raised my head to look at Edgar. He'd returned through the front hallway and was standing over the body again, examining the scene. There was no direct suggestion of a cover-up, no overt implication in his voice to do anything wrong, but the question in and of itself raised the possibility. Maybe there was some way of spinning what had happened here to make it look like Rebecca didn't commit murder.

"No." Rebecca's voice was low and clear with a sense of conviction. "I know what you're thinking, Jerry Strickland, and I love you for it, but the answer is no. You need to call this in or whatever it is you normally would do. I killed this man and I won't be asking for any special treatment."

I glanced over my shoulder at Edgar, who was biting his lip and shaking his head.

I look back at Rebecca. "But what you just told me "

"What I told you won't make any difference in the end, will it?"

I said nothing.

"I can tell you've already been thinking it through."

I looked again at Edgar. "Give us a couple of minutes here, will you, Ed?"

He nodded. "We've got to hurry up and do one thing or the other here, Jer. She just confessed."

"I know she did. I know."

Edgar took one last look around and out the windows as he backed out of the room. I turned back to Rebecca.

"Do you know what you're looking at here?"

Her tears had stopped for the moment. "I'm sure it's horrible. I'm sure you're about to tell me how horrible."

"A charge of first degree murder, which you just admitted in front of Edgar. A sentence of twenty to thirty years, maybe life. We can prove Gramm was a bad guy. We can prove he murdered Jackie Brentlou. Maybe there are even others, I don't know. But what we can't prove is what's in your head, as much as I believe in it, as much as we both may know it's true."

"He would have killed others too if I hadn't stopped him."

I sighed. "I know."

She put her hand to her mouth, lowered her head, and started to cry again. "We can't tell them any of this though, can we, Jerry? Any of what I saw."

I shook my head. "They'll label you. They'll put you through all sorts of psychiatric evaluations. They'll have you looking like one of those people who murder abortion doctors."

"What else can we do then?"

I looked again at the gun in my hand. "This is my gun. We can make it look like I did it. At least I can build a plausible motive."

She was already shaking her head. "I can't let you do that, Jerry."

"Why not?"

"It isn't true."

"Neither is keeping silent."

"I know." Her eyes cleared for a moment. They seemed to have a far-off look to them.

I rubbed my hand across her shoulders. *"I can't stand the idea of you being charged with murder. Of you going to prison for this."*

She reached up and took my arm. *"Jerry, there's something else I need to tell you."*

"What?"

"About the girl he was stalking, the girl he was about to kill."

"Yes?"

"She's someone close, Jerry."

"What?"

"Don't you see? You couldn't have known because she was too close."

I watched her for a moment. *"What are you talking about? Who was it?"*

She looked away from me, her eyes straight ahead, her face set in stone. *"It was our Lori,"* she said.

• • •

Colin sounds far away. He is asking me which way to turn, but it feels like I am in a dream. My arm throbs some, but it's mostly gone numb, which I know is not a good sign. Time seems to be slipping away.

"Dad said Seminole Hill. Do you know where that is?"

I nod my head up and down to clear it. "It's a shopping center down the street. Turn right and look for the signs."

"Here it is," he announces, barely an instant later, it seems.

I look up to see the front of the Saab turning into Seminole Hill shopping center. It's been years since I passed by here, but I still remember the place: a drab collection of stores in a dated strip mall, the main anchors a busy supermarket and a drug store. At this time of night, grocery shoppers fill virtually all of the parking spaces. Seminole Hill is a good place to slip in and out of without attracting attention, if that's what Harper has in mind.

We drive around the side of the main building. Even more cars here, overflow from the front. But there among a row of additional stores stands a defunct knitting shop just as Alex described, looking dark and vacant with its front window and door covered over by brown paper and masking tape. A travel agency next door is already closed for the day.

Colin manages to find a space to park the Saab parallel to the curb.

I reach for the handle and push open my door. For the moment at least, I don't try to stand. "See if you can borrow a cell phone from someone. Tell them it's an emergency and get 911 on the phone."

I just hope Alex was right about Marnee being here and Harper hasn't already moved her somewhere else.

A minute later, Colin returns, accompanied by a middle-aged woman with a kindly face. "I'm already talking to 911," he says. The woman looks down at me with concern. I'm the emergency, she must assume.

"Great work, Colin. Thank you, ma'am. I'll take the phone."

"Sir, you should be asking for an ambulance."

I look down at my arm. She's right. I'm losing more blood.

"In a minute."

Colin hands me the phone.

"Mr. Strickland?" I hear the operator's voice.

"I'm here."

"This is Shawana with emergency dispatch. Your grandson has already filled me in. I have Henrico County PD in route."

"How long, Shawana?"

"Five minutes. Maybe less. We working an accident with fatalities on the expressway."

"Understood."

Five minutes. It might be too long.

"I've been told we have a potential hostage situation."

"That's correct."

"Your grandson also tells me you're a detective and you've been shot."

"RPD. Long since retired. And yes, I've been hit."

"Are you armed?"

"No, ma'am, not anymore."

"They're advising me to instruct you to wait for the officers then. Wait for backup."

"Okay, Shawana." My head feels fuzzy again.

"You don't sound convinced, detective."

I smile. Shawana must be an old pro, accustomed to reading the inflection she picks up in her callers' voices. "I'm just tired, Shawana. Just tired."

"Stay with me, detective. Stay with me."

A faint burst of light flashes from the back of the store.

"You see that?" Colin says.

I nod.

"Detective?" The dispatcher must have heard Colin's voice.

"How much longer, Shawana?"

"Three minutes out. Four tops."

The light flashes again. Someone is definitely inside the vacant store.

I look across at Colin, covering the handset with my palm. "We wait three or four minutes and Marnee and your father may be dead."

"Did you say something, Detective?"

I put the phone back to my chin. "We've got lives in peril, Shawana."

"Copy. Lives in peril."

"I can't wait. I'm going in."

Thirty-Eight

Lassiter's hands are slick with sweat as he drags the bleeding man—this Alex, this pathetic excuse for a father—across the back of the darkened store toward the man's daughter. She's still where he left her with her hands and legs bound and her eyes closed. The place smells of mothballs and fabric glue.

Lassiter needs to be done with all this, so he can move on. His choices are all gone. His plan hasn't materialized the way he hoped, but he should have enough cash in the end. All that's left to ponder is the manner of the kill. What is he waiting for?

He chuckles to himself, and it occurs to him, as if from a distance, that it's not his own voice he's hearing, but the maniacal laugh of Jacob Gramm from the night at the motor court years before. Predatory, like a starving hyena.

Gramm's voice is joined by others. Some better, some far worse, scratching fissures.

Lassiter can't seem to shake them from his mind.

• • •

"But, sir—" Shawana is nothing if not persistent, but I ignore her. Would have liked to had a chance to meet her.

I brace myself against the car seat. "We're parked right in front," I say. "Tell them to look for the old Saab, a young man and a woman. I'm giving the phone to my grandson now."

"Hold up."

But I miss whatever else Shawana has to say. I'm already pulling myself to my feet and stepping from the car.

"What's happening?" The woman with Colin cringes as she gets a better look at my bloody arm.

"Just stay here with my grandson, ma'am, and wait for the police. Keep behind the car. Colin, you too."

"What?" Colin raises his arms. "Granddad, wait up. I've got to go with you."

"No, you can't, buddy. You need to keep this line open and watch over this fine lady. Stay here and wait for the officers."

"But—"

"End of discussion." I turn and push out as quickly as I can. Unsteady at first.

"I love you, Granddad." I hear him over my shoulder.

"Love you, too." It comes out as a whisper and I don't look back.

Stepping up to the storefront window, I slip to one side and flatten myself against the frame of the plate glass window. Daylight is dwindling. The front door to the shop is only a couple of feet away. I reach across and try the handle. It's locked, of course.

I pause, listening for any sound. Nothing at first, but then I hear voices and what sounds like a man's muffled pleading. Alex.

No time to think it through. I rise up, ignoring the searing pain in my side, and lift my heel, kicking with all of the strength I have left at the glass lettering that reads KNITTING.

It's not going to work, I think, I don't have the strength, but the glass breaks apart with a boom, shattering and splintering to the ground. To my left I catch a glimpse of someone moving: Rebecca again. A shot rings out, the bullet pinging against the top of the window frame. The woman behind the car with Colin screams.

I go in low, fighting with my hands to prevent becoming entangled in the brown paper. What remains of the dim light floods through the window with me, but is quickly swallowed by the darkness inside. Another shot, and I roll to the floor, scrapping my knees and injured arm against the thin commercial carpet. A solid brick countertop covers half of the entryway and I scramble behind it. At least I've given Harper something else to think about besides Alex and Marnee.

The shooting has ceased.

I peer around the side of the countertop.

The scene at the back of the store looks like something out of Dante's Inferno. Shadows fill the empty space, but somehow I can see enough. Marnee lies bound and gagged on the floor, unconscious, asleep, or drugged, I hope.

Not dead. *Please, don't let her be dead.*

Harper is standing against the opposite wall with the gun still pointed in my direction. Not expecting any company, he's leapt to cover behind a pair of shipping barrels. Alex is prone on the floor between him and Marnee, bleeding but still breathing.

"Well, well. Detective Strickland?" Harper calls out. "Jeez, you're a tough old bird, aren't you? Takes one to know one."

"It's over, Harper. Let's end this. Turn yourself in."

"Yeah, right. How'd you get out of the office?" His voice sounds more panicky than before. Panicky and dangerous.

"I had a little help." That ought to make him think. "What have you done to the girl?"

"Oh, she's fine. A sleeping little princess."

The truth? Or bargaining for leverage?

"You're by yourself, aren't you, detective? I don't see any SWAT coming crashing through the window. The kid with you, too?"

"You've only got a few minutes to live if you don't give it up now, Harper. The cavalry's on its way." A faint siren sounds from somewhere in the distance. Harper says nothing. I'm sure he can hear it, too.

He laughs, but it's no longer the laugh of a man in control of the situation. "Wow." His voice is lower, talking to himself. "How'd it all come down to this?"

The storefront is silent for a moment.

"I can still walk out of here with hostages," Harper shouts.

"Not if we can help it," a voice whispers from somewhere behind me.

I turn to look and smile.

It's Lori, with Hal Ford and Colin.

They take cover to one side of the window. Ford is toting a twelve-gauge shotgun.

I've never been more glad to see anyone in my life.

"You're a hard man to keep up with, Jerry." Ford's whisper is raspy. He keeps both the shotgun and himself out of Harper's line of vision. I can see the three of them from where I crouch, but Harper is blind.

Lori looks across at my tourniquet. "Dad, you need a hospital."

Harper calls out again: "What about it, Detective? You up for a little hostage taking?" He's not giving up.

I speak to Lori under my breath. "What I said about the story I'd written down?"

"Yes?" She nods.

"It's in a false bottom in one of my dresser drawers at the house. Show it to the newspaper editor David Wilhelm, too."

"All right."

"You still with me, Detective?" Harper's voice is growing more agitated.

"I'm still here," I call out to him.

There must be a back door, which is how he got in and how he plans to leave with either Marnee or Alex, maybe both, in tow. Sounds like he's getting ready to move.

I look at Ford.

"He doesn't know you're here," I whisper.

Ford nods.

"I can draw his fire, get him to focus on my motion and make him shoot low. You can lock in on his barrel flame. He won't see you coming."

No, Dad, Lori's eyes plead. "There must be another way."

The sirens are getting closer, but not close enough.

It's all making sense, everything Rebecca tried to tell me. Because after she started working with me, she wasn't the only one having visions of my cases.

I was seeing them, too.

And I'm looking into the darkness again, clear as a bell.

"There's no time." I look back at Ford.

He and the Feds must have at least suspected, which is why they wanted me out of the way. They'd all heard stories about what happened with Rebecca.

"Don't try to follow us, Detective!" One of the barrels scrapes along the floor as Harper moves.

Ford's gaze locks on mine. "Put a slug center mass?"

One last look at Lori and Colin. A silent prayer and I nod.

"Do it."

Epilogue

Two months later

The first hints of autumn appear on a warm breeze in Richmond. The sun gives up its summer intensity. A subtle change inhabits the trees. The nights come sooner, too. It has always been my favorite time of year.

Lori, Colin, and Marnee make their way across the grass in the late afternoon light.

Marnee wears a white dress under a blue sweater. She still limps a little, but it's barely noticeable. Her mother has picked out a matching bow for her to fix in her hair, and she is holding her brother's hand. For his part, Colin has on a collared shirt and his hair is cut shorter. In his other hand he carries a bouquet of flowers. Lori is decked out in an attractive skirt with a matching jacket. She carries flowers as well.

The stones hug the edge of a small grouping in a private corner near a granite bench. The two monuments lay side-by-side, one showing less wear than the other, otherwise identical except for the differing names and dates.

When they reach the spot, Lori stoops and places her bouquet beside the first stone, while Colin follows suit with the other.

Something sweet buoys the air, a stillness and a glory.

Lori looks down at Marnee. "What are you thinking?"

"I miss grandpa," she says.

"I miss him, too, sweetheart. I miss them both. It's a shame you two never got to know your grandmother."

David Wilhelm has run a series of articles in his newspaper based on my memoir. They've put a whole new spin on Rebecca's decades old case.

Tears well in Marnee's eyes, not for her own fear and pain, I understand, not for the bad dreams she will have to endure, but for the future missed kick of a soccer ball, the silly grin on the grandfather left lying in the darkened storefront beside her.

"Maybe one day we'll get to meet her, and get to see Grandpa again, too," Marnee says.

"You know what?" Lori drapes an arm over each of their shoulders. "I think we just might."

They look at the stones and smile.

A gust stirs the fresh flowers, a turn in the flash of light.

And I almost wish they could. I wish they could see Rebecca and me, the two of us riding the wind again, with her arms wrapped around my waist, like we did on my Harley Davidson along the Blue Ridge Parkway for all those years when we were young.

END

ACKNOWLEDGMENTS

No matter how obsessed I become, whether writing a book or flying a hawk, my wife and children reel me in. They love me and they put up with me, though they know me best, grounding me in ways I need. My wife and older kiddos are also my first readers, which is extremely helpful because they all like to read— a lot.

Beyond them, for the creation of this story I owe particular thanks to the Moseley Writers Group, my long time compatriots in the struggle to make our writing all it's meant to be. Others—Judy Bushkin, agent Scott Miller, John David Kudrick, author Ken Kuhlken and my classmates in the master's program at Perelandra College—provided valuable critiques. Cindy Davis gave stellar copy-editing support. The Richmond Police Department was kind enough to allow me to go on a ride-a-long. And Deputy Commonwealth's Attorney Rick Moore offered some important advice about legalities surrounding a charge of murder.

As usual, the responsibility for any mistakes, technical or otherwise, is mine and mine alone.

ABOUT ANDY STRAKA

Publisher's Weekly has featured Andy Straka as one of a new crop of "rising stars in crime fiction." His books include A WITNESS ABOVE (Anthony, Agatha, and Shamus Award finalist), A KILLING SKY (Anthony Award Finalist), COLD QUARRY (Shamus Award Winner), KITTY HITTER (called a "great read" by Library Journal), and RECORD OF WRONGS, hailed by Mystery Scene magazine as "a first-rate thriller."

Andy has worked as a book editor, movie production accommodation agent, commercial building owner and consulting vice president for a large specialty physician's practice, surgical implant and pharmaceutical sales representative, college textbook sales and manuscript acquisition representative, web offset press paper jogger, laborer on a city road crew, summer recreation youth director, camp counselor, youth basketball coach, assistant parts manager at an auto dealership, assistant manager at a McDonalds restaurant, and even been registered as a private investigator. (Not to mention a longstanding stint as a stay-at-home Dad to six, which makes neurosurgery look like tiddlywinks.)

A licensed falconer and co-founder of the popular Crime Wave at the annual Virginia Festival of the Book, Andy is a native of upstate New York and a graduate of Williams College where, as co-captain of the basketball team, he "double-majored" in English and the crossover dribble. He lives with his family in Virginia.

CPSIA information can be obtained at www.ICGtesting.com
Printed in the USA
BVOW01s0859200514

353970BV00001B/6/P